DAMNATI
LOVER'S
LEAP

The Jamaican Legend continues

By Horane Smith

PublishAmerica
Baltimore

First printing

ISBN: 1-4137-8404-6
PUBLISHED BY PUBLISHAMERICA, LLLP
www.publishamerica.com
Baltimore

Printed in the United States of America

For Beverley, Jabez, Freda, Alton, Pearl,
and the people of Yardley Chase

ACKNOWLEDGMENTS

Many thanks to Joylene Griffiths-Irving and Noel Scoburgh for their invaluable assistance; Rita and Sam Burke for the encouragement; my family for giving me the time; and to my readers who kept asking for this sequel.

CHAPTER 1

Her eyes were swollen, red, and ugly. Anita Campbell looked pitiful, visibly shaken, yet she couldn't imagine she had any more tears left to cry. She had shed more than enough, after twenty-five miserable and tormented years of grieving for her slave lover Jerome Scott. But she was mistaken this morning, as the tears kept coming. Anita wanted to weep, and she was weeping. The tears rolled down her cheeks with ease; she allowed them to flow freely, first a slow streak, and subsequently they let loose as if they would never stop. She felt the warm drops bouncing off her dress and onto her shoes.

A surge of wind whirled from three miles below, and blew right across the peak at Lover's Leap on Jamaica's southern coast. It brought a stinging sensation to Anita's face, parting her blonde hair to reveal bone white scalp. The impact of the wind in her eyes forced more tears. She turned her back to escape its wrath, although it made no difference. In fact, if she hadn't grabbed a small tree beside a protruding rock she would have been toppled by the force of the wind.

The rock, which was flat at the top, was the favorite place at Lookout, the area that later became known as Lover's Leap, at Yardley Chase, in the parish of St. Elizabeth. In 1830, exactly twenty-five years ago today, Anita's lover, a young slave, jumped to his death from the rock, along with another slave, Alice Walker, after their secret love triangle had been discovered. Since then, it took on the name Lover's Leap. The love triangle was forbidden on all fronts. It was never meant to be because it was a love for tomorrow, not 19th century Jamaica, under British colonialism.

Perhaps it would have been different for them now that slavery was no more. Emancipation was announced in 1833, three years after Jerome and Alice's suicide, but became effective fully in 1838. More than three hundred thousand slaves became free men and women. The post emancipation period had promised revolutionary changes—Anita and Jerome's only hope—but he never lived to see that day.

The gush of wind died a slow death within a few minutes. Anita stepped back onto the rock wiping her eyes, as she stared at the angry waves three miles below, the memories of the past gnawed at her mind. The awesome beauty of the view from the cliff didn't captivate her anymore. The beauty was there, yes, but for Anita, it was agony and grief whenever she came there to recollect the memories.

The sky was cloudless on this April Sunday. One oval frame of blue joined the almost indistinguishable horizon, adding more color to the turquoise waters of the Caribbean Sea. Looking east, several miles of the island's rugged coastline were clearly visible, as it came under its daily battering from huge waves. Westward, the cloudless sky made it much easier to see a fifty-mile stretch of land along the winding coast.

More tears rushed into Anita's eyes as soon as she reluctantly recalled that fateful day when her lover, and his other love, hurled themselves from the cliff. Anita sat on the rock to relieve the light feeling in her head. She clasped her hand, stroking her hair to prevent it from falling into her wet face. What a misery life had become for her over the years. She lived in daily torment, and Anita had started to wonder if it was her punishment for nurturing the forbidden.

The ordeal was too much to bear after the fall; the recovery of the bodies, the disorganized burial, and the disgrace she brought to the family. The relationship with her parents, Alfred and Lynda, had been strained ever since. They should have retired already. However, Anita sensed that, because of what happened with Jerome, they were reluctant to pass on the plantation to her. John Stewart, the overseer, seemed destined to inherit some powers. He, too, had become a bitter enemy though he still wished Anita would stop living for the dead—a dead slave at that.

Twenty-five years meant little to Anita's physical features. She remained a beautiful woman. It was hard to guess her age. Her gift from the sun, evenly tanned skin, gave her an exotic look that would be the envy of anyone coming from the colonial master—England. Her evenly curled lips and sparkling brown eyes would turn any man's head. Nevertheless, the only head she wished she could turn at this moment was Jerome's. But he was dead, long dead.

"You're remembering again, Mom?" said a voice that caught her off guard. Anita turned quickly to look directly into the eyes of her son, Andrew. He could see the swollen eyes, the tinge of red around the eyelids, the long streak of tears crawling down the side of her cheeks. "When will you ever get over this, Mom?"

"I don't know, my son, I just don't know," she said, trying to hide the fright in her voice. She wished Andrew hadn't seen her like that. She tried hard to avoid him whenever those sad moments brought tears. Andrew must have seen her like that at least a hundred times over the years. Anita loved him to death. For one, he reminded her of his father; that was the only piece of Jerome she could hold onto. Andrew was Jerome's son, Anita's only child, illegitimate, and the son of a slave and a white woman, a mulatto.

It wasn't difficult to tell that he was of mixed race. He was a light shade of black, with a handsome face like his father. However, his brown curly hair gave him a slight resemblance to his mother.

"It's time you do, Mom," Andrew said, coming up to her.

Anita looked up at her son, admiring his maturity and the confident tone in which he spoke. "You're right. I should've forgotten him long ago. The way it ended keeps haunting me," she said softly.

Andrew peered out into the deep blue of the Caribbean Sea. A flock of seagulls flew beneath the cliff, the whiteness of their feathers glistening against the greenery of the forest below. The seagulls seemed so happy, yet he could see the tear-filled eyes of his mother slipping away into a world of grief and torment. He made one step forward to come closer to give her a hug.

The sobs burst out of their silence, dripping tears onto Andrew's shirt. He felt them soaking through his shirt and onto his skin. Those were the tears of both parents, he thought. Andrew wanted to cry, too, but he braced himself against that. As a man who must provide comfort to his mother, he must remain strong, he told himself. He withdrew from her grip when he heard her sobs no more. The two of them sat quietly on the rock staring over the cliff, the thought of a lover and a father blanketing their minds. When would this grieving end?

"Ah, my coffee is cold, Lynda," said Alfred Campbell, Anita's father and the owner of Jack's Place, the second biggest plantation in the area. Larry Daniels had the biggest in tobacco. Jack's wife Lynda had just made him breakfast. Jack, who had been very sickly over the past ten years, had become somewhat absent-minded. The coffee was given to him hot. All that time he sat around the table looking out through the window toward Lover's Leap. Something was on his mind.

"Is anything wrong, Alfred? You seem a little uneasy?" Lynda asked.

"I'm fine," he grunted. Jerome's foster mother, Maude, his father figure, Babwe, their main help around the house, had died in the past two years. Lynda took on some of the household chores and had to be contending with the likes and dislikes of Alfred. The older he got, the more difficult she found it to cope. The estranged relationship with their only child, Anita, hadn't made matters any better. On top of that, since the suicide of Jerome and Alice, life had never been the same. Guilt had become a bitter enemy. Lynda had been slowly accepting that. Alfred and John Stewart, the overseer, had a long way to go in getting over that guilt.

A blue curl of smoke slipped in from the kitchen. Elsa, a slave, was working in the kitchen, but had to rush out to fan the smoke away. The small piece of dishcloth she had in her hand was useless. She knew Alfred and smoke weren't friends. "Sorry, Massa! Sorry, Massa! De wood hard fi burn," she blurted out apologetically.

It was too late. Alfred had started to cough. The coughing got so uncontrollable that he had to go outside for a breath of fresh air. Anita and Andrew came up the steps at the same time. "Are you okay, Dad?" she asked.

Alfred stared at her. She had been crying again. He could see the swollen eyelids. "I should be the one asking you that question," he said as soon as the cough eased.

Anita turned away her head. Andrew remained silent. They knew another argument was brewing.

"Good grief, Anita! When are you going to bury that slave once and for all!" he yelled, stomping his feet as the coughing started again. "Look around you, woman! Yardley Chase...Big Yard can be yours one day if you could only get yourself together..."

An answer wouldn't be a wise thing, Anita thought.

Alfred believed she had gotten over Jerome. Only moments ago, he was peering through the window thinking of a time when Anita was in charge, married to a strong and hardworking man. He was faced with the reality once more that she was still grieving. The last time Alfred had seen her cry was about two years ago. She had stopped visiting Lover's Leap for a while, but she went back today. That visit must have triggered off something. *When would this nightmare end?* Alfred wondered as he stormed back into the house.

Lynda watched him come back in, after overhearing the encounter with Anita. She, too, was taken aback with the revelation that Anita was crying again. She followed Alfred into their room.

"We're getting on in age, Alfred. Anita has to come to grips with this, but how?" she said, as if she was talking to herself.

Alfred sat down on a chair beside his bed. He looked out into the blue sea as it faded away into the horizon. A cool wind was blowing through the window, dividing the white curtain.

"That's a tough question. I thought she was over this slave long ago. His bones have long turned to dust and she's here grieving. Can you believe that? My goodness! This is incredible! This is madness."

"I hate to say this, Alfred," Lynda replied, not looking at him, "but Anita truly loved Jerome."

"Hmmm," he sighed, staring at the floor.

"We can deny it all we can. The proof is there. We saw it again today, it doesn't make sense deny it."

"What does that mean?" he asked curiously. Lynda looked at him. He had wrinkled very quickly. Alfred's entire head was white, nevertheless it matched quite nicely with his heavily-tanned skin color. She wished he could enjoy his senior years much better than how he was doing. That was a goal she aimed to achieve.

"It can only mean one thing," Lynda said.

"And that is..."

"We probably need to do something at last. We have to resume the idea of finding her a husband," she said.

"John Stewart is out of the picture, I presume," Alfred said, standing up to walk around the room.

"Yes, for sure."

"Then who? Do you have someone in mind?"

"As a matter of fact I do." Lynda smiled.

Andrew was passing his room and couldn't help but overhearing the dialogue between his grandparents. As soon as their voices faded to silence, he walked quickly up to his mother's room. Anita was sitting on the bed with the Bible in her hand.

"You've turned to that now, Mom?" he asked, pointing to the Bible.

"Hmm, that's all I have, son...apart from you, that's all I have. My parents are against me. I've no one else to lean on but Jesus," she said, caressing the cover of the Bible.

"You better brace for more trouble from them, Mom."

"What do you mean?" she said, turning around to face him.

"Maybe I shouldn't tell you this."

"I've been through a lot already…might as well you say it. My heart is drained of all my emotions, there's hardly any left, my son."

Andrew stepped backward and shut the door behind him. A squeak from its rusty hinges signaled that it was shut. "Um…you won't be lonely for long."

"Dad has some more plans for me, right?" she asked, forcing a smile.

"How did you know?"

"I know them too well, son. They've been trying to force John on me from day one."

"Well, he's out of the picture," he teased.

"They said that? I wonder whom they have in mind. By the way, where did you learn all of this, Andrew?"

"Open doors with voices always have a story to tell." Andrew smiled. "They don't always close their door when they're talking."

"Maude was good at hearing what she shouldn't have heard. May God bless her soul," she said with reverence.

"She was a good woman. I miss her terribly. There'll never be another one like her," Andrew said, walking over to sit beside her on the bed.

"Never say never. The former slaves live in appalling conditions and we may see someone like her soon, and we'll have to reach out like we did with Maude."

"I would welcome that, Mom. That's why I have to get out of this area," he said calmly.

"What? Get out? What do you mean?" Anita asked, looking at him all over.

"It's hard to tell you, Mom, but it's something I have to do…"

"What you have to do?" she asked, anxiety building up in her voice.

"Go to Kingston," Andrew said dryly.

"Kingston? Why Kingston? It's far from me here, Andrew. I'm alone, you know that," she said, anxiety in her voice.

"Politics. I have to fight for the ex-slaves. I want to sit in the House of Assembly some day. My father was a slave, he died a slave. Aunt Maude and Babwe were free but they never really enjoyed freedom. Slavery was abolished yet there's no real improvement for ex-slaves. They don't even own land to begin with. How can they ever have a life without land? I want to see improvement. I'll work for that until the day I die. I owe my father that," he said emphatically.

Anita was quiet for a moment. The walls of her stomach burned from the sudden stress that came over her. She rose from the bed and walked over to the window. The huge star apple tree known as Hell House, the very tree under which she had met Jerome the night he was sent there for punishment, stood sturdy and imposing. It seemed like it had never aged. It was laden with leaves. The shade it provided was a welcome relief during the hot and humid days.

Anita didn't want to revisit the scene that first night she had met Jerome. The memories were too painful. Instead, she measured the tree with her eyes, from its bulging roots to its very top. It was very sturdy, strong and had weathered the hot days as well as the cool nights. Hell House had acted as a shield for her and Jerome in their clandestine encounters. Anita wanted her son to be strong and confident in what he was doing. Most of all, he should never be confronted with a need to hide anything he was doing.

Anita stared at the floor, trying to get her thoughts together before answering. "Your father would have been proud of you, Andrew. He dreamed of freedom so we could be together, but he never saw that day. Do what you have to do, Andrew. I'll have to survive without you."

Andrew's eyes were glossy from tears. He hugged his mother. "I'm not quite ready yet, Mom. I'll let you know when. I would prefer to hang around until things are sorted out around here."

"Please don't wait for that, dear. It could be a long wait."

"I won't abandon you, Mom," he said, rising from the bed. "I'll not leave you in this mess. You know what, probably you should come with me." He grinned.

"Where? Kingston?"

"Yeah," he quipped.

"Hmm, this is home for me, son. I think I'll die here."

"Don't talk like that, Mom. You're a young and beautiful woman. You only need to go out to meet people."

"I know that would help but for the time being it's not in my thoughts. Let's forget it for now," Anita said, trying to convince him everything would be alright.

John Stewart was convinced he would inherit part of Jack's Place. Alfred entertained that idea whenever he was confused about Anita's future. John had been a faithful overseer all his life. He had endured the tough times on the plantation. It was logical for him to look forward to his reward. At one point in his life, he thought Anita would be that reward—a wife. That was only in his dreams. Anita despised him even more after Jerome's death. The few times Alfred saw them speak he detected resentment.

The afternoon sun was losing its intensity. It had been a hot day. It was the opportune time for an afternoon walk. Alfred decided to do exactly that. He couldn't take his afternoon nap because of the discomfort of the heat, so he decided to pay John a visit.

John was trying to rescue some tomato plants from the weeds when he saw Alfred walking along the edge of the garden toward him. He was glad to be able to stand upright. The short time he was bending to snatch out the weeds, his back started to hurt. John's protruding stomach was certainly not a plus for him in this instance. It made bending very difficult. He would start to sweat profusely after a short walk. It was no surprise that he rode his horse wherever he was going, be it near or far.

A few strands of gray hair drew a line in his mustache, while a few others were clearly visible in his whiskers. John was more than lonely. The few women coming from England all seemed to have taken up residence in Kingston. A south coast parish like

St. Elizabeth hardly saw any of them. He was becoming more desperate as he added on the years. He hated the idea of returning to England, having grown accustomed to the warm climate.

"Poor tomatoes," Alfred said as he approached him, "these are killer weeds," he groaned, stooping to pluck one locally known as Sleeping Mary, out of the ground.

"They'll survive. I'll ensure that they do," John grinned.

"Uh-huh, I'm sure you will."

"Is everything okay?" John asked.

"I guess so. We have to give God thanks for life each day. It could have been worse. We've come a long way together, John."

John waited with abated breath, hoping to hear something that would maybe cheer him up. "I've done my best, sir."

"You've done that, John. I'm grateful for that. I need your help again."

"Oh m'boy, you're in demand." John smiled internally, wishing he could beat his chest in triumph. "Anything I can do, I'll do, Alfred, you know that."

"Somehow this may be a bit different, John. You may not enjoy hearing about this," Alfred said, bending down to pull some more weed from around a plant.

"I'm listening." He kicked a small pebble at his feet, sending it over to the other side of the garden. John was nervous.

"It's Anita."

"Anita? What about her?" he asked.

Alfred knew John's love for his daughter had never faltered. It would be very painful for him to say what he wanted to tell him. He decided to test the waters first. "Are you still interested in her?"

John's eyes were fixed on the ground. He couldn't look at Alfred; he preferred not to at that moment. "I can't deny I love her to death...she has no feelings for me, Alfred. I couldn't live with that pain again after I've gotten over her."

"I'm sorry about that. We did try. You know that. We wanted that badly."

"I know, Alfred," he said, looking at him.

"Would you be willing to help her?" Alfred asked abruptly.

"Help her? How?" he asked, a little startled at the question. "Settle down."

"I don't understand, Alfred," he said, bewilderment all over his beefy face.

"I need to find her a husband." Alfred felt awkward to say it like that, after John's relentless efforts in the past to win her had failed miserably. "She needs one badly. The years are going by. She knows it. The time for her is now."

For John, it was like the sharp horn of a bull had pierced his heart and there was no blood spurting from it. He scratched his elbow, the dirt from the soil leaving its stamp of visitation. John's mind was in turmoil. "A husband?" he said in disbelief.

"I guess so. I think this is your right time, John. "

John raised his eyebrows. "Me? Are you sure?" he asked, wanting to smile.

"I'm positively sure, John," Alfred told him.

John didn't want to show his shock. The moment Alfred's mouth uttered those words, the first thing John thought of was whether he should have another attempt at winning the woman of his dreams—Anita Campbell. Yes, she hated his guts. In Anita's eyes, Jerome's death could easily be blamed on him. But time could mend a broken heart. After all, they were rather close at one point in their lives; so close the subject of marriage came up.

John knew Anita was still thinking of Jerome. That didn't deter him from having another try. One thing John thought he had in his favor: Anita was lonely more than ever, so was he. Would desperation triumph over resentment? That was a gamble John Stewart was willing to take.

CHAPTER 2

The absence of free labor had taken its toll on Jamaica's number one crop—sugar. Sugar had been king for many years. How long would it be able to hang onto that coveted position? That was a bet many plantations were reluctant to challenge.

Former slaves toiled in the cane fields daily, with the hope of earning something to live on. It was no easy task. Some of them wondered what emancipation was all about. Life was a brute, despite the fact that they were no longer the property of a slave owner. They wanted land because it could open many doors that had already been closed. The shackles of slavery haunted them menacingly, both mentally and physically, bringing dark clouds on their horizon.

Wilfred McIntosh, a British citizen, was the Minister for Yardley Chase Baptist Church. It was a small congregation of about thirty people. The pastor was a popular figure in the community, as he ministered to the sick, the dying, and the living. He was forty years old; he towered to over six feet into the sky. Many villagers had to stare up into his face while talking to him. Pastor McIntosh was a noticeable handsome man with blue eyes, carrot-looking hair, a round face, and a small pointed nose. He was a hard worker, and as humble as one could be. At least, that was what he had been told many times by members of his congregation.

Sunday morning came with a certain aura in the atmosphere. The whistling wind that was sometimes heard coming up from Lover's Leap wasn't there today. The air was placid, its freshness like the mist hovering over a mountain stream. It was a day for worship, and the congregation came with that in mind.

Pastor McIntosh was in the mood for worship. He had only been in Jamaica for two years. He felt at home already. He was well-respected, called upon for advice from all and sundry— from the rich to the poor, from white to black. The pastor was fulfilling his expected role in the community.

Pastor McIntosh was standing at the door of the church welcoming his guests. Two surprise visitors were standing before him face to face. He knew them. However, as far he could remember, it was the first time he had seen them in church. Anita Campbell and her son, Andrew, stood before him with outstretched arms. They couldn't help but notice his hesitation.

"Surprise, Pastor?" Anita asked timidly.

"I've to admit I'm a little, let's say, startled," he chuckled. "But I must add quickly that it's indeed a great pleasure to have you both here," he said, smiling.

"We're glad to be here," Andrew said, releasing his hand from the pastor's firm grip.

"We've been wanting to do this for some time. I guess there's a time for everything," Anita said.

"Ecclesiastes 3:1...there's a time for everything," the pastor said, almost laughing.

"I can see you're ready to preach," Anita said. "We need to hear that more, sir, that's why we're here."

"Jesus will never abandon us. He never will. As long as we give our lives to Him and trust in Him, salvation is assured. It's a great pleasure to have both of you with us today. I look forward to the day when your parents will be here, too." He smiled.

Alfred and Lynda gave financial support to the church, although they never attend services. The pastor visited them on a few occasions as a mere courtesy call. Pastor McIntosh was always praying for them in his daily word with God. As for Anita, he knew of her troubles in the past, the difficulty she had in trying to get over Jerome. She never requested any spiritual guidance from him, he never attempted to give her any. It was like the two were avoiding each other. Yet, here she was today—at church. He was rather interested to learn more.

At the pulpit, Pastor McIntosh delivered a very compassionate sermon on what he had told Anita: Jesus Will Never Abandon Us. Anita had to admit that the sermon did something for her. It was as if she had someone to turn to now, someone who understood her troubles, most of all, someone whom she could rely on.

"It was a touching sermon, Pastor," she told him at the door as he greeted his departing visitors. "I could relate to it. I guess I need to start asking myself some questions."

"The Holy Ghost works mysteriously, my dear. Jesus never fails. Anytime you feel like talking to someone about the saving grace of God, I'm here," he said, extending his arm.

"I'll certainly be taking you up on that, sir. I certainly will." Anita smiled.

Andrew listened carefully. Somehow he was convinced that God had answered his prayer regarding his mother. She was about to make a change in her life.

A flash of lightning divided the afternoon sky, thunder followed, rolling and roaring across the dark, gray sky. Within seconds, the heavenly blessings came pouring out of the sky in huge drops. The rain battered the dusty ground, breaking the short drought that had been affecting most southern parishes over the past three months. The smell of dust was overtaken quickly by the freshness of rainwater that was pouring out harder and harder. The crops were smiling, plantation owners, farmers and even overseers like John Stewart.

John was smiling at the fact that the drought was no more. But equally so, he was also jovial about something else. He was smiling about his just concluded decision to make one more try to win Anita. John, you're one handsome chunk of flesh, more than two hundred pounds of it, and you can win over Anita this time, he told himself convincingly. You have the skill John, like the overseer you are, so what could stop you? There's no Jerome this time. John, you're the winner, he said, almost aloud. John thumped his chest in anticipated triumph.

From the corner of his window, John watched the long streaks of water from the sky absorbed by the tobacco and cane fields across from his house. They reminded him of the tears he cried many nights for Anita more than twenty years ago. Oh! He was young and hotheaded, he said to himself. Anita was like that, too. She should be more receptive now that they both had matured.

John told himself he needed a planning strategy. He would take his time, although the days were moving by quickly. The grays reminded him of that, but he must start right away.

The gray and chilly afternoon turned to evening. Then Yardley Chase was engulfed in darkness. The night would be rather cool and Anita hated that. Why? There were many nights, she re-called, when she wanted to be with Jerome and all she could do was cry until she fell asleep. Her pillow would be like a wet towel.

Anita couldn't sleep tonight; she went over what had happened during the day. Church was indeed a blessing. Her troubles seemed to have vanished for as long as she was there. Even afterward and up to this moment, she was in a much better mood. She thought of Andrew's notice of departure soon, and told herself that rather than discouraging him, she would have to do the opposite. Andrew had to do it for Jerome. She reversed her thoughts back to church. They would have prayer meeting or something like that tomorrow night. Next Sunday was rather far away, at least that was how it appeared; why not make use of another opportunity before that, she contemplated. Anita fell asleep on that thought.

The sprawling mansion of Jack's Place had weathered the storms, from the turbulence of slavery right up to the time of emancipation. Slave labor had built this imposing structure. Empty stomachs, while growling for lack of food, had carried rocks, wood, mud, gravel, limestone and water to build the mansion. Andrew remembered the stories on how Babwe's father worked hard on it to get it finished. There were days, Babwe had told him, when not even the heavy showers could stop the work. The first task was to build a stone wall around the property. When that job was done, all the slaves who worked on the wall were left with huge blisters on their hands.

The construction of Jack's Place was a proud accomplishment of the slaves, worthy to be told to their children and grandchildren. That story, along with the now infamous suicide at Lookout, renamed Lover's Leap, would be told for generations. Andrew was a product of that first generation.

Andrew had grown up on the plantation of his grandparents. His interaction with former slaves or their descendants was quite limited. Everyone in Yardley Chase knew or heard about his father, Jerome. However, he commanded a lot of respect from the black population, primarily because of his mixed race as well as the wealth of his grandparents. Although he was a mulatto, Andrew was treated like any other white person on the plantation because he happened to be kin; he spoke and acted like he was white.

Of late, Andrew had been exploring some ideas spinning around in his head, regarding the adaptation of the former slaves in the area to the new political landscape. They needed a voice because they had none. Could he be that voice? Andrew had been asking himself that question for some time now. He would be twenty-one soon, and the time to answer that question was fast approaching.

Interaction! That was what he needed to do more with the community. Perhaps church attendance was the first step indeed. Anita liked it, he could tell, and that was another bonus.

It was mid-afternoon and Andrew was standing in front of the huge iron gate before his grandparents' house when two young men, older than him, came walking by a narrow track a few yards away.

"How yuh doin', sah?" one of them said.

Andrew knew him as Jeremiah and had even spoken with him on more than one occasion. "Fine, Jerry. How about you...and Simon?" he asked, referring to the other man.

"Time is hard, sah. We need lan' fi wuk so wi can eat, Massa," Jeremiah said soberly.

"We waan' to wuk fi wi self, nat fi anybody," Simon said seriously.

"Come, let us sit and talk," Andrew said, beckoning to them to come by the gate. There was a stone wall leading up to the gate that would make a comfortable seat. "Are you in a hurry?" Andrew asked.

"We have de time, Massa. Anyt'ing dat can mek life betta fo' us we haffi to talk 'bout it," Jeremiah replied, sitting down beside Andrew.

"I know the problems you're all facing. You can't survive on nine pence. You don't have enough land to plant your own food and to sell the rest at the market."

"Right, sah, yuh right," Jeremiah interjected, looking into Andrew's face as if he had the solution to their problems.

"Apprenticeship didn't bring about some of the things you need. It didn't put slaves on the right footing. I'm lucky I grew up in a decent house because my mother is white. Your houses are leaking and there aren't enough rooms for your children."

During the period of apprenticeship from 1838 to 1840, slaves had to work three quarters of the work-week for their masters for free. The rest of the week they could work for wages and for themselves.

"Yuh is correc', sah. Is dere anyt'ing yuh can do?" Simon asked.

Andrew looked down on the ground. "I have some plans. They probably won't come to fruition right now, but I want you to be aware that I'm going to work for the betterment of all former slaves," he said confidently.

"Yuh have little color sah and dat mek yuh have a better chance a getting t'ings done." Jeremiah grinned. Jeremiah was in his mid-twenties, broad at the shoulders and smaller at the waist. He looked strong and ready to work. His sparkling eyes had a determination to succeed. Simon, too, appeared muscular and agile. He was about five feet eight inches, and from all appearances, was a hard worker.

"Men like yuh is what dis country needs fi get out of dis mess," Simon said.

"Slavery seems to be lingering around. I can see some plantation owners are spitefully not employing former slaves. It's like they want to get back at them. I won't stand for that. Thank God my grandfather isn't like that," Andrew said.

"True, sah," Jeremiah said.

"But he can't employ everybody around here because the tobacco market isn't as big as before. England isn't buying much sugar and tobacco from us these days. The other islands are shipping sugar there, too. I hear of some plantations in the west employing laborers from abroad and hard workers like you are here working on and off. I have to fight for this to stop," Andrew said, clenching his fists.

"Yuh soun' like dem important man from Kingston, sah," Jeremiah said.

"Right, sah," Simon echoed in agreement.

Andrew wished they were right.

A huge full moon rose stealthily from behind the Spur Tree Hills, and lit up the darkness of Yardley Chase, with a bright silver glow. As the moon crawled from behind the hills, its orange tint slowly disappeared and silver took over, as it gained height and spread its sparkling rays over land and sea. Before its arrival, the night was pitch black and was very discouraging to anyone who would want to take a stroll. Trees, shrubs, fields, houses and even the face of John Stewart glittered from its bright rays.

It was just a few hours into midnight. John had retired to bed early because he didn't get much sleep last night. Tonight was no better.

To his chagrin, he rose from the bed and walked over to the window to be greeted by a silver moon. He was amazed at the brightness of the surroundings. In years gone by during slavery, he would have been wary about going outside at that hour of the night. He had lived with the nightmare of a possible slave uprising for many years. He didn't feel like that anymore with slavery being abolished. The night was ideal for a walk.

John had a notion that Anita was the reason for not wanting to sleep. During the heavy downpour last night, he had started to think about Anita. Imagine that! After many years of heartaches over Anita, he was again caught in her web. There was a time when he thought he had definitely got over her. There was no doubt about that.

Alfred's visit was what changed everything. The latent feelings that John had for Anita, had resurfaced again. One of them was jealousy. Since last night, thoughts of Anita tickled his brain, and he could think of nothing else but to win his life-long battle for her.

John put on some clothes and stepped out into the cool night air. The rich resonating voices coming from the church, a few yards up the road, filled the quiet night with an enchanting melody. He came out in time to hear the final line being sung. Up above, the stars twinkled in their glory, and to the east, the shining moon would be his accompaniment for the night. He changed his mind about walking up to the church, after the singing had stopped. He could hear mumbling voices, a signal that the mid-week meeting was over. A few people walked passed his gate within the ensuing minutes. He remained in the shadows, preferring not to be seen. John wasn't much for church; he wanted it to stay that way.

John's house, which he built five years ago, was small compared to Alfred's imposing and somewhat intimidating structure. It stood right across the road from his employer. He did that deliberately to keep abreast of his job of overseeing the whole plantation. Tonight proved there was an added benefit.

The woman he had been agonizing over was the same person he recognized coming down the road in the buggy. There was someone riding behind them. It took him a few seconds to realize that something was wrong with that scene. The proximity of John's house to the road made it less challenging for him to recognize the person sitting beside Anita. Andrew wasn't that tall, and the mode of dress could only belong to Pastor McIntosh. The person behind on the horse was undoubtedly Andrew.

What's going on here? John mumbled to himself. What's the pastor doing with her? He lived in the opposite direction. Surely, he couldn't be going over to see Alfred. He turned to watch closely, as the buggy turned into the gate at Jack's Place, and drove up to front of the house. They had been the last ones to leave the church. Hmm, John you better investigate, he told himself.

John opened his gate and walked to Alfred's house. The sound of horses' hooves on the solid pavement alerted him. He dashed behind a clump of bushes to avoid being seen by the rider. Pastor McIntosh rode passed him, disappearing into the night. *What was all that about, John m'boy?* he wondered. Was it just a friendly visit? Anita had fooled her in the past with her nightly flings with Jerome. Was she up to something again? There were too many questions. He needed more answers before it was too late.

Meanwhile, Anita was surprised Pastor McIntosh offered to see them home safely. It was an offer she couldn't refuse. Her second visit to church was indeed another blessing for her. She was more at ease and life seemed more meaningful. At times, guilt came to mind. She wondered if some of the things the pastor was saying were meant for her. The general terms in which he spoke made her felt otherwise. That made church more homely for Anita.

Admittedly, Anita was totally mesmerized by his near presence during the short ride to her house. He had offered to ride beside her. Pastor McIntosh spoke at ease, with a confidence in his voice that shattered her doubts about things physical as well as spiritual. Pastor McIntosh was the epitome of a wretched sinner, who had repented and accepted Jesus as the Deliverer, the Savior. She wished she could speak like that. During that short ride, she hastily concluded that it was someone like the pastor whom she needed to help her heal the wounds of a broken heart. If Jesus was entering her world, the pastor could easily help her to find Him. If she must let go of Jerome, Pastor McIntosh could be the person to help her. There was little difficulty in arriving at such a conclusion.

The good times she had with Jerome had become burdensome—a load to heavy to bear. Her parents were totally fed-up. She could see that Andrew wished for a change, too. He would be gone soon, and Anita would become lonely again, much like the period before she met Jerome. There was no way she could allow that to happen. Anita needed Jesus; she was convinced. Pastor McIntosh was only too willing to help her find Him.

Anita went up to her room then returned to the living room to make a cup of tea. She sat in a chair beside the window admiring the bright moonlight. The former Hell House, the seat of punishment for Jerome and other slaves, looked ghastly in the moonlight. Tonight, she must resist the memories it brought of days gone by. It would be a new beginning for her from here onward. Tomorrow, she would walk to Lover's Leap to tell Jerome one last goodbye. Andrew drew her chair nearer to the window, parted the curtain, before staring into the heavens. Was Jerome up there with the Heavenly Father? Maude, Babwe, Alice?

Goodbye, my love, she said to herself, remembering her pledge to Jerome never to look at another man. But Jerome was no longer alive, and the time had come to move on. *We will meet again; this time it will be under the rule of God. There will be no slavery, no sorrow, no pain.* "Thank you, Jesus," she said aloud.

"Are you alright, Mama?" Andrew asked softly. She didn't hear him come up behind her. Anita was startled at first; however, being so familiar with that voice, there was nothing to fear.

"I'm very fine, my son."

"I was almost certain I heard you talking to someone," he said, pulling a chair to sit beside her.

"Maybe I was doing that without even being aware of it." She smiled.

"But who were you talking to? Is someone out there?" Andrew asked, rising from the chair and looking through the window like he was expecting someone.

"Never mind, son, it was all up here," Anita said, smiling and pointing to her head.

"Your imagination?"

"Yes."

"Is it my father again?" A curious look came across Andrew's face, clearly visible in the dimly lit room. Anita's heart raced faster. She became nervous.

"That was the last time, Andrew...I'm certain it was the last time," she said, looking out into the night in the direction of Hell House.

"The last time for what, Mama? What are you talking about?"

"I'll go to Lover's Leap tomorrow to bid your father goodbye." She came over to him and began rubbing her hand in his hair. "I've got to get on with my life. I have you. When I have you a piece of Jerome will always be with me. That, I have to be thankful for."

"I'm glad you see it that way, Mama," he said, hugging her.

"He was the love of my life, will always be. Nevertheless, life goes on for both us. We have to make the best of it because we're only here for a time."

"Well said, Mama, I'm proud of you. Please don't you forget that Pastor McIntosh is here for us. He'll supply all our spiritual needs."

"Well said, son." She smiled, wondering why he brought up his name.

CHAPTER 3

Andrew's pet, Teddy, was an eight-pound rooster, whose bed was the thick limb of a small breadfruit tree beside Alfred's house. Teddy rose from his sitting position, muscled up, and blew his signal loudly to indicate the dawn of a new day. His crow echoed across Yardley Chase.

The other roosters followed suit in less than a minute. They joined in unison to send a wake-up call to all and sundry. Teddy crowed thrice, a ritual that the community had come to rely on to know when it was time to rise and shine.

John heard the crows. He was somewhat delighted to jump out of bed after a night of tossing, turning, and haunting nightmares. He wanted to start work early, hoping to pay Anita a surprise visit late afternoon. He must move quickly if he wanted to be out front. Pastor McIntosh could be a formidable foe or a friendly rival. On the other hand, he could merely be a harmless, innocent preacher, trying to minister to a lonely sinner.

Andrew could be used as a kind of bait to get to Anita, John thought as his heavy boots splashed into the soft mud that paved the walkway to his house. He looked up into the sky only to see nothing but blueness. It should be another good day in the field, provided there was no rain later. All his plans should fall into place, he hoped. *John, you're an expert*, he told himself. He would even be a better expert if he could start having a better relationship with Andrew.

John resented him mainly because of his resemblance to his father Jerome. John's agony was anything that reminded him of the slave who stole his woman's heart. With his renewed quest to win her once more, John would befriend even an enemy. Andrew was far from that.

John deliberately walked over to Jack's Place before going to the field. Andrew would be up feeding the chickens and Teddy that time of morning. He was right.

"Isn't it a beautiful morning?" a delightful John mused, coming up behind Andrew who was busy throwing corn to the hungry birds.

"Huh, you almost had me there. Never thought I'd see you around here this time of morning," a teasing Andrew said, already sensing that wherever there was smoke, there was fire.

"Hey c'mon, Andrew, many times I pass you here, said good morning and you didn't even notice me." He grinned. "Look out there!" He pointed in front of him at the misty surroundings. "With such beauty I have to make sure you hear me this morning."

"Well, I can only hope that when it's raining you'll be here to help me feed the starving," he said.

"You bet I will. In fact, anytime it rains I'll be here before you, I guarantee," John boasted, very pleased with the opportunity to make up for lost ground. He could barely hide his conquest in that regard.

"Hmm, you seem pretty happy this morning, John. You must have slept like a baby last night, or is it something else," Andrew said, eyeing him cautiously.

"You're right…it was one of those nights when sleep was far away and you were wishing that morning would come. I was glad when Teddy woke me up."

"I still don't get it," Andrew answered, somewhat puzzled.

"Ha! Ha! Ha! M'boy, there're some things a man would prefer to keep to himself, especially when he knows for sure that it's bound to happen."

"Uh-huh, sweet dreams?"

John smiled from ear to ear. "Sweet dreams becoming reality," he said sheepishly.

"I'll wait for that to celebrate with you," Andrew teased again.

John's face lit up. "Celebrate you will, my dear boy. It'll be one grand celebration for all of us."

"All of us?" Andrew asked, wondering what this was all about.

"Indeed all of us. I won't say more. You do have a good day, m'boy," he beamed, walking off to the tobacco field.

"You remember your promise that whenever it rains you'll be here first," Andrew called out to him.

"Don't you worry. I'll do that with all pleasure."

Strange indeed, Andrew thought. *Very strange indeed.* If he knew the conniving, unpredictable, and slimy character that was John Stewart, something must be up his sleeve. Andrew was determined to know more.

Peter Bradley was glad to take the long ride to Yardley Chase. He got word from Lynda that Alfred had business to discuss with him. The hard-working barrister had been handling their legal affairs for many years. Lynda had met him on one of her many trips to Black River, the biggest town in the area. He was the right person she was looking for. Instead of going to Malvern, a smaller town that was nearer, Lynda preferred to go to Black River.

Peter, who had turned forty recently, was a medium built and rather refined Englishman with sparkling eyes and a perfectly shaped face. It seemed his nose and mouth were placed at the right spot. But for a man living in the tropics, his skin lacked sunlight because he worked indoors. He dressed well, making him appear like an aristocrat; Peter was far from that. He earned good wages and made an effort to make himself presentable to his clients.

Alfred had been adding the years, which gave Peter no second thoughts about the reason for his visit. *At long last,* he thought, *Alfred had decided to re-draft or make amendments to his will.* He remembered distinctly that the first one he did had omitted his beautiful daughter, Anita—someone whom Peter had always admired. Her crime; she was once in love and bore a child for a slave. Alfred must have had a change of heart, he theorized.

The barrister rode most of the way from Black River. He stopped only a few times to give his horse a break. His trek across the Pedro Plains was quick encountering little difficulty. He would be climbing a little higher soon, to enter the Santa Cruz mountain range that would eventually end up and descend into Lover's Leap.

Peter had visited Lover's Leap on two occasions in the past two years. He thoroughly enjoyed his visit on both occasions. Somehow, he had a gut feeling that his impending visit would even be more enjoyable. The message he got from Lynda didn't say much, except to say, we need you here urgently. On the last visit, Anita acted as if she knew she wasn't destined to inherit any of her father's estate. She didn't say it in as many words, nevertheless, it wasn't a problem for Peter to decipher that out. *Anita's undying love for that slave must have finally been put to rest,* Peter thought. *The future looked bright for her.*

Peter rode into Yardley Chase late afternoon. Lover's Leap was known for its breathtaking sunsets and this afternoon was no different. The western portion of the sky was lit with an orange flavor. The clouds lining the horizon appeared to have gotten their share of color and had passed it on to the others fading in the background. The few patches of blue in the sky added to the spectacular scenery created by the dying sunlight. The ripples of the waves stretched all the way from the shore to the horizon dotting it with its share of orange.

The sunset caught Peter's eye, and he diverted from the road in order to take a look over the cliff at Lover's Leap. It was the first time he would see a sunset from the peak. He couldn't miss this one.

"Who...h-hey, you startled me," Anita shouted, jumping to her feet suddenly. Peter steered his horse right up to the edge of the cliff. The whistling wind coupled with the depth of her thought, made it almost impossible for Anita to have heard anything. She didn't recognize Peter at first. "Oh! Peter! What are you doing here? You're the last person I expected to see," she said.

"Hi, Anita. I'm so glad to see you. How are you doing these days?" he asked, trying to speak above the noise of the wind coming from below.

"I'm doing fine, Peter. How about you?"

"I'm okay. I was riding to your house, saw the sunset here, and decided to take a look. I've never seen it like this before. Look there," Peter said, pointing from along the horizon, "isn't that truly the perfect example of how beautiful nature is?"

"It is, Peter. Lover's Leap is truly a beauty. One day this place will be a major attraction for many people. It's too beautiful to ignore." She smiled.

"They'll wonder how it got the name, too," he said softly, wishing he hadn't said that. "I'm sorry, I shouldn't remind you of the memories," he said, lowering his voice. The tone told Anita he meant it.

Anita paused before answering. She glanced down at the roaring raves below, before looking up at Peter. "I came here today to bid goodbye to Jerome, Peter. I've decided finally to bury the memories. I'll always love him. I did love him to death. There won't be another like him...today I begin anew."

Peter saw the tears building up in her glossy eyes. He came over to hug her. She hugged him back, remaining in that position for about a minute. "I think it's time you do, Anita," Peter mumbled, hoping the tears had ceased.

"Thank you, Peter," she said, releasing her hold.

At the same time, a pair of cold eyes squinted between the leaves of the thick shrub bordering the stones near the peak. The eyes couldn't believe what they were seeing; they turned away from the object then looked at it again. The picture was the same as before. With shock and dismay, the face that owned the eyes pulled away from the space it occupied between the leaves, lowering its body to the ground in a crawling position. As a Jamaican yellow snake would do, the body wriggled between rocks and smaller trees until it got closer to the object.

John Stewart wanted to hear the dialogue between Anita and the person he recognized as Peter Bradley, Alfred's barrister. At first, John thought it was Pastor McIntosh. But the clothing gave him second thoughts. On his way from work, John had seen Anita heading for Lover's Leap. He had been hoping for an opportunity to talk to her in private. He had hurriedly changed into some better clothes and headed there, too. John saw the horse as he approached the cliff. Anita had walked to Lover's Leap. The sight of the horse meant she had company. John came in time to see both of them hugging. He felt jealous.

"I know it has been difficult for you over these years," Peter was saying.

"I cannot deny that," she said.

"You've shut many people out of your life, Anita," Peter said sincerely.

"I know. I know I've made life difficult for people like John," she said calmly.

John? She said John, came the muffled croak from beneath the nearby bushes.

"John is a good man, Anita. He would've made a good husband."

"I know he's a good man. Let's go to the house, Peter. Some other time we can continue this conversation," she said, turning her back to the spot from where Jerome and Alice leapt to their deaths.

"As you say, ma'am."

Anita never bothered to even ask Peter what brought him to Yardley Chase. Perhaps it was better she didn't ask at this stage.

They left a puzzled, sweating and uncomfortable John slumped to the ground. He was relieved when they left the scene. What he had witnessed in the last few minutes had given him much to think about. Peter's visit was certainly on his mind, and what Anita had said about him was surely more pleasant than anything she had said to him in the past twenty years. *John, you have won this day,* he said to himself. He was right about what he had told Andrew that morning.

John crawled out from underneath the shrub, his legs and hands cramped from lying in one position too long. He yawned lazily, pondering his next move. The plans to have a talk with Anita had to be shelved. The words that came to his ears this afternoon gave him some comfort; however, he felt uneasy and admittedly troubled by Peter's visit.

Meanwhile, Andrew had been bored to death all afternoon. He saw his mother leave for Lover's Leap. He knew she was about to do as she had said—bury the memories of his father. He stood by his bedroom window all afternoon, looking out into nowhere. Suddenly, something caught his eyes. He watched two figures come into focus as they strolled up the pathway to his grandfather's house. He knew one was his mother and assumed that the other was Pastor McIntosh. He could think of no one else. Andrew wanted to go out to meet them. On second thoughts, he changed his mind when he glanced at them again, recognizing the person as his grandfather's barrister.

Andrew wished there were times he could sit to have a lengthy, interesting conversation with his grandparents. His relationship with them was as estranged as his mother's ongoing struggle for a change of heart. He felt strongly that, as long as he lived, they would never accept him as a grandson. Anita's cardinal sin was to give birth to the son of a slave—once the property of Alfred.

Their grandson was like a stranger in the house. That was why Andrew was convinced he had to leave to make a life on his own. Furthermore, there were too many injustices being meted out to the newly freed slaves, he thought. That was his passion: to bring equal rights and justice to the oppressed and underprivileged. He had heard of other freedom fighters in the parishes of St. James, St. Thomas and Kingston. He wanted to join them, to eventually sit in the House of Assembly, sooner rather than later. First, he must ensure that Anita would be fine without him.

Andrew scratched the side of his head. There seemed to have been a turn for the better in the past couple of days, as far as his mother was concerned. The pastor had been steering her in the right direction. The pastor could help this barrister, too.

Andrew had been watching the way Pastor McIntosh looked at his mother. Maybe Andrew was wrong, or could he have mistaken lust for admiration? Peter was visiting again out of the blue. Was the visit to nourish a relationship with his mother, or was it to finalize his grandparents' will? Better yet, did this visit have anything to do with Lynda's pledge to find someone for his mother? There were more questions than answers for Andrew. He was tired of scratching his head. A slight headache bore through his forehead.

Lynda was elated to see Peter. He marched right into the living room, his heavy boots pounding against the wooden floor. A faint smile came across her face; Alfred stared at him with a blank expression. Peter's eyes combed the room before coming to rest on Alfred. Undoubtedly, he had aged a bit since the last time he saw him. The wrinkles were more pronounced; he had less hair. The look on Alfred's face brought home one message to Peter. He wasn't expecting him.

Lynda jumped quickly to greet him. "Oh! I'm glad you're here," she said, winking her eyes at Alfred. She hoped he wasn't frightened by the visit. Anita, who was in the room, couldn't have seen that gesture. Peter saw it and he picked up something unusual.

"Uh, it's always good to see you, Peter. How was the trip?" Alfred mumbled.

"I did it in record time." He grinned. "With no rain, it was smooth sailing all along the way."

"You must be hungry. Supper is ready and waiting," Lynda said, pointing the way to the kitchen.

"I certainly would do with some food," Peter replied.

"Anita, please join us," she said, whispering softly into her ear. Anita rarely ate with her parents. The dinner conversations often times turned into bitter disagreements, often times a quarrel, and eventually malice. Anita ate with her son on most occasions in order to maintain the peace. She detested playing the hypocrite this evening.

"Is Andrew invited?" she asked dryly.

Lynda hesitated; it was useless to argue now. "If you wish."

"And no quarrels," Anita said, almost pleading with her.

"There'll be no fuss if you say the right thing."

"I'll keep quiet, Mom. The war has got to stop."

"You mean that?" Lynda whispered, almost entering the kitchen.

"I've found Jesus," Anita whispered back.

"That's the best news I've heard in a long, long time," Lynda said.

There was a knock on the front door. Lynda dashed for the door, anxious to see who was knocking. The burly figure of John grinning his tobacco-stained teeth, took up nearly the entire doorframe.

"Hello, Lynda."

"Hi, John, is something wrong?" she asked rather hastily.

"No, ma'am. I wanted to tell Andrew that I'd feed the fowls tomorrow morning." He grinned, trying to look inside at the same time.

"Oh! That's nice of you, John."

"Mmmm, something smells good in there, ma'am."

Lynda knew John was nosing around for news. He must have seen Peter.

"I'll tell him for you, John. I'm certain he'll be happy to hear," she said, without even acknowledging his compliments. "You have a good evening now."

"Okay, ma'am," John said, in almost a whisper.

John was bitter. His anger boiled uncontrollably and his face reddened; turning, he walked down the steps without even looking back. Lynda saw his reaction and wished he hadn't come. She wanted Peter's visit to be perfect. Somehow John could be a threat. Poor John, she almost whispered aloud, he always seemed to end up getting the wrong end of the stick. She regretted Alfred had ever spoken with John about Anita, without discussing it with her. Lynda was adamant that Peter, rather than John, be given an opportunity with Anita. Alfred had protested initially, deciding afterward to go along with Lynda's choice reluctantly.

Lynda returned to the kitchen to find Andrew and Peter in one deep conversation. Alfred sat across from them at the table, disturbingly quiet. Normally, he would be chatting away with his guest; he could have been upset by Andrew's intrusion.

"Are you okay, Alfred?" Lynda asked. There was no answer. "Alfred!" she called again, raising her voice.

"Uh a...Oh! Where were you?" Alfred stuttered, after being taken off guard. His mind was far beyond the room. It must have wandered off into the heavens, and back to earth.

"Oh! He's alright," Peter said, ending the conversation with Andrew. Anita walked in at the same time.

"Are we ready to eat?" Anita asked.

"We are ready," said Lynda, relieved that John had left.

Anita surprisingly volunteered to grace the table. Alfred and Lynda exchanged glances. Peter looked impressed.

"I can see you have God in your life," Peter teased.

"In fact, I'm trying to these last days," she replied, a smile rippled across her face.

"You're going to church?" Peter asked, sinking his fork into a piece of beef.

"I am going. The Baptist Church is just over there," she said, pointing through the window behind her.

"That's encouraging to hear, Anita. You can soon start preaching to the sinners like us," he grinned. "By the way, your stew is good, Lynda."

"Thanks, Peter. It was done in a rush; I'm glad it's edible."

"How have you been keeping, Alfred?" Peter asked, turning to look at him.

Alfred looked up from his plate, trying to finish the food in his mouth before he spoke. "I guess I'm holding on. I may soon have to start visiting church to make peace with God, too." Alfred meant what he said, however, the way it came across made the others thought he was joking.

"The years are going by, my dear sir. What better to do than live according to the Word of God?" Peter said.

"There goes the word of a preacher," Lynda chuckled.

Anita didn't like the tone in which the conversation was going. It sounded like mocking God, but to preserve the peace, she remained silent. Andrew glanced at her. He knew right away that Anita didn't like the tone of the dinner conversation.

Anita walked outside for some fresh air after they finished the meal. Peter followed her quickly.

The stars were peeping out from deep space. The heavens were a twinkling covering of blackness mingled with millions of lights, forming a marvelous spectacle to the naked eye. There was no moon tonight; the stars would rule in their glittering splendor.

Darkness had covered Yardley Chase. A faint beam of light shone through the window from Alfred's living room onto Peter's face, as he stood before Anita in the dark. Anita thought he looked quite handsome with the light only shining on one side of his face. She found herself being pulled into his embrace before they could even begin a conversation. What appeared incredible to Anita was the reality that she didn't resist his hold.

CHAPTER 4

A deathly silence slowly engulfed the village of Yardley Chase. It was the silence of sleep. All souls, the weary and the tired, were in their beds; even the animals had retired early.

There was no noise from barking dogs, croaking frogs, or whistling crickets. John Stewart was the only living thing making noise. His snore sawed steadily, disrupting the silence in the room. It continued in the same vein, except for a few brief disruptions, until during the wee hours of the morning when John jumped to his feet clutching his throat. He was having a nightmare. John dreamt that Peter was trying to strangle him. He woke up sweating profusely.

An angry John had stormed away from Lynda and rushed into his house. He sat there thinking Lynda was right not to invite him in for dinner. They must have wanted some private talks with Peter, whatever that meant; he didn't want to hazard a guess. John felt like he always ended up getting dirt. Sometimes he was on top of everything he wanted, while other times he was a sore loser.

John parted the curtain to look outside. A new day was dawning as the glare on the horizon emerged in the eastern sky. He recalled his promise to Andrew. There was no way he could return to bed; it was a good time to sniff around. The best way to do that was to fulfill his promise.

John had almost finished feeding the chickens when Andrew showed up. He couldn't believe his eyes when he realized John was almost done.

"Well, well...good morning, John."

"Hey! Look who's here. It's certainly a good morning, Andrew—at least for me. How about you?"

Andrew rubbed his eyes. "I'm alright."

"That doesn't sound too chirpy." John grinned. "It sounds like you didn't get any sleep."

"I did, although the house was a little busy."

"Oh. Hmmm, you had a visitor?"

"Yes."

"If you're going to be up every night like that you're in for a rough week, m'boy," John said dryly, attempting to get some information on how long Peter would be there for.

"I hope not. I surely hope not."

"If that's the case you should avoid the conversations...if that's the problem."

Andrew knew John had started fishing for information. His political sense told him not to go any further. "It's not a problem, John. In fact, I do welcome the company...the extra words."

"I see. Well, at least you can't say I haven't kept my word here." He pointed to the chickens gobbling up their corn.

"You have and I'm grateful. Had I known you were out here I wouldn't bother to come."

"I would've left a message with the maid, but I didn't want to be seen around the house that early."

"Why? You're helping me out," Andrew declared.

"Hmmm."

"Is something wrong?"

"Ah! M'boy, I hate to say this...your grandmother..."

"What about her?"

"The fact is I came by last night to tell you I was going to feed the chickens. She told me she would tell you. I had planned to stop for a few minutes but I could see Lynda didn't want me around," John said, looking away from Andrew's stare.

"What? How come?" he asked.

"I guess because of the visitor," John said, waiting for his reaction.

Andrew frowned a bit before he answered. "Uh-huh, Peter. I see."

John looked up at Andrew, wondering what was running through his mind. Andrew remembered the conversation he had overheard between his grandparents regarding the loneliness of his mother. Did his grandmother organize Peter's visit? The answer was almost clear to Andrew.

By the time Andrew returned to the house, a ravenous Peter was already devouring breakfast. Andrew joined in time to hear Lynda's comments.

"You haven't eaten for days, Peter."

"You're right, ma'am. On top of that, these Johnny cakes are a treat," he grinned, his teeth crunching into one of them. Andrew was quick to notice that his mother was sitting right beside Peter. He felt awkward, opting to sit on the other side next to Lynda.

"Good morning, Andrew," Peter said between mouthfuls.

"Good morning, Peter."

"You get up this early every morning?" Peter asked.

"Teddy reminds me when it's time to get up."

"Who's Teddy?"

Everyone around the table smiled at the question.

"His pet rooster," Anita laughed.

"You did it quickly this morning, Andrew," Lynda said.

"I had some help."

"Who?" Lynda asked.

"When I got there John fed them already."

"John?" Lynda said alarmingly.

"John the overseer?" Peter asked.

"Yes," Andrew said.

"That's one dedicated worker, Alfred. I've never seen his second," Peter acknowledged.

"You're right. John has been my other hand all these years," Alfred said.

"Would you like to go for a ride?" Peter asked Anita after breakfast.

"Where to?" she responded.

"Anywhere other than Lover's Leap." He forced a smile.

"I can see you don't like it there? Yardley Chase is a big district, we can go anywhere you want. Furthermore, I won't be going back to Lover's Leap for a while."

"You hope to keep that promise, right?"

Anita paused before she answered, searching his face to determine what he was thinking. "That's right."

"Well, let's go for a ride to the neighboring district."

"Top Hill? We can even go to Junction or Southfield, wherever you want." She smiled.

"The horses are ready," Lynda interjected. She was coming through the main door in time to hear the conversation. It was exactly what Lynda wanted to hear.

They rode away from the house in a slow trot; slow enough for Pastor McIntosh to recognize Peter from the back of his house, where he had been trimming the hedge. He had met Peter on his last visit to Yardley Chase. He didn't bother to question the reason for his visit. That wasn't his business. Pastor McIntosh was more concerned about Anita's spiritual needs.

Anita broke the silence ten minutes into the ride. The horses were trotting slowly while Anita had been gazing at a nearby field, as the songs being belted out by the laborers caught her ears.

"That sounds very good," she said. "The sun is scorching and they're singing. Isn't that lovely?"

"I always like to hear those folk songs. Sometimes they don't make much sense but there's a certain melody they have that makes it almost impossible not to listen to them. That's one legacy they have carried over from slavery."

"I'm glad slavery is over; these former slaves still have a far way to go. They need someone to fight for them."

"I agree. The timing is right, too."

"Andrew wants to do that."

Peter almost tightened the reins. "You mean that?"

"Yes. He's dead serious. He wants to fight for the freedom his father never had," Anita said, her eyes not leaving the tobacco field.

"Hmmm. That's a just cause. That means he'll be going soon."

"Yes. I'm trying to face that right now. I see it coming."

"I guess you can only encourage him."

"I have to...I have no choice. My greatest challenge will be to remain at home with my parents with no one around to really keep me company."

"It's time that relationship improves," Peter said, looking her straight in the eyes.

"Why are you here, Peter? Did my mother ask you to come?"

Peter almost fell off his horse. The question struck him like a bolt of lightning. He thought quickly of a way to avoid answering directly, but with Anita, he knew it was futile. Anita was good, exceptionally good, at digging for answers.

"She did ask me to come here. Both of them did."

"Why?" They had passed the tobacco field. There were no more songs to hear. The horses moved a little faster on the narrow road. Stones, holes and a bumpy surface were the obstacles in their way. Peter and Anita didn't need to guide the horses to walk at the best spots. They knew them already.

"Hmmm. I'm under cross examination," he said, watching the horses manoeuver their way through the best part of the rugged surface.

"If that's what you're thinking, it must be so."

"Alfred and Lynda are moving on in age as you know..."

"It's the will. Isn't it?" she asked, rather demandingly.

"I guess you can say that."

"What do you mean? Is there something else you're not telling me?"

"I-I..."

Both of them pulled up their horses under a lignum vitae tree. Its thick cluster of leaves provided the right shade.

Underneath the tree, the grass was crispy from the scorching sun. Peter was the first to dismount. Anita was reluctant to get off the horse, forcing Peter to hold her hand to help her down. Before her feet could touch the ground, Peter slid her into his arms and their lips met.

"That's why you came?" Anita mumbled.

"Yes," he said, releasing her. Both of them sat on the grass enjoying the shade. "I want to kill two birds with one stone."

"Two birds?"

"Figuratively, yes. The other bird, so to speak, is to find out from Alfred if he has made his last will and testimony. Not that I'm interested in his will. I'm interested in you, Anita...since my last visit you've always been in my mind."

"Really?" Anita blushed.

"As his barrister, I want to ensure that he takes care of his family before it's too late," he said, holding her hand.

"Does that include me?"

"You're his only child. The will..."

"It doesn't include me?"

"It's not for me to say. Let's say there can be some improvements to it."

"Mom doesn't have anything to do with the visit?"

"Yes and no. She thought it's time I pay another visit to ensure everything is okay."

"My mother is a good woman, despite our strained relations. However, sometimes she does things on impulse. I've a funny feeling, Peter, your visit is one of such responses," she said politely.

"You know your mother wouldn't do anything to hurt you."

"I know that. I think my mother likes you," Anita said with a smile.

"I think she does," Peter said, pulling up some weeds beside the stone he was sitting. He threw them into the road. "Women are like weeds."

"How so?"

"They are happy one minute; by the next they whither away in sadness."

"Hmm, we can't be happy all the time, especially when life gets boring and empty."

"Like yours?"

"Not really. Mom wouldn't mind having you for a son-in-law, right?" she asked bluntly.

Peter admired her for her openness. She spoke from her heart. He hoped she could be as open as possible with his next question. "Are you going to prevent that from happening?"

The ripples on the surface of the Caribbean Sea could be seen clearly stretching away toward Lover's Leap, from where they were standing. It was a beautiful view. The Pedro Bluffs glared at them about twenty miles away. Despite the haziness, the scenery was a feast to the eyes. Anita hadn't seen them from that angle before; her eyes were fixed on them.

"Aren't you going to answer?" Peter followed her stare.

"Oh! It's so beautiful here. What a view!" Anita exclaimed.

"I've never seen it from here. It's truly amazing."

"You're amazing, too, Peter..." Anita wasn't certain why she had said that. Even before she could allow any possible reasons to come flooding into her mind, Peter sealed her thoughts with a kiss. At that moment, another funny thing happened. Anita's thoughts raced as fast as they could to a smiling Pastor McIntosh.

Jeremiah watched Andrew walk up to the dilapidated house his parents called home. He had lived there all his life. Jeremiah's father, Abraham, had worked all his life on Alfred's plantation. He worked on it from the days of slavery through emancipation, right up to this very day. He was one of the laborers Anita heard singing a few minutes ago. His mother, Mammi, had died about a year ago. Jeremiah's two younger sisters, Mary, eighteen, and Sally, twenty-one, were sitting with him under a mahagony tree beside the house. They were two beautiful girls.

The house was built from wattle—a mixture of dirt, twigs, and limestone. It was small with two rooms: a makeshift kitchen was at the back. Cracks in the side of the house suggested the walls needed some repairs. The thatched roof was firm enough to keep out water no matter how heavy a downpour.

It was Andrew's second visit to Jeremiah's house.

"What breeze bring yuh here, Massa?" Jeremiah teased, getting up to shake his hand.

"A strong one," Andrew said, grinning. "How are you, Sally...Mary?"

"Fine, sah...fine...alright."

"Glad fi see yuh, sah. Is everyt'ing alright? Here, yuh sit dere," he said, pointing to a little wooden bench beside Mary and Sally.

"Oh! Thank you, Jerry. How is everything going?"

"Caan' be anywhere worse, sah. No work...Dat's why mi sittin' down yah."

"I know it's bad out there. We need some more opportunities in these parts. In the east and the west, even up north, it may be a little better, although we hear of disturbances."

"Disturbances, sah?"

"Yes. Some very brave men in St. James have been struggling for work and better working conditions for ex-slaves."

"Hmmm. Somet'ing is happening then, sah."

The two girls listened attentively, somewhat amused at their brother's interest in the disturbances.

"It will be a long struggle, Jerry. I think I may have to join soon."

"You soun' like an important man already, sah. Yuh should be over dere fighting fi us. We need s'mebody up dere, sah."

"Yuh serious 'bout dat, Massa Andrew?" Sally asked.

"I'm thinking about it."

"Dat would be good fi us, sah. Wi in a slavery still," Sally said.

"I know the feeling. I agree something has to be done and very soon, too. Those cabbages look pretty good, though," Andrew said.

"De girls tek care a dem, sah. Wi can get some fi yuh when dem ready."

"Thanks, Jerry."

"Yuh waan' some coconut water, sah?" Jerry asked, looking up into a nearby tree.

"That would be refreshing."

"Mary, go fi mi machete."

Jerry was up in the tree within minutes. The coconuts fell to the ground the moment he reached them. He picked about six before he came down to open them for his visitor. Andrew couldn't go any further after drinking the first one. He stayed for about two hours, talking, laughing, and repeating some old jokes about slaves and their slave masters. It was a refreshing visit for Andrew. If, and when, he left for Kingston, he might not have another opportunity like that to talk. He would always remember this visit.

A new day had dawned on Yardley Chase. Yesterday, it was fun for Peter, today it would be a hard day's work. Lynda was pleased with Peter's visit, so far. Her plans had been working out perfectly. The other part of the plan would be a test of Peter's ability to win over Anita. Getting Alfred to change his will to include his daughter and grandson could be a formidable task for Peter. Lynda knew she couldn't convince him to do that; it would take Peter's legal persuasion to succeed.

"Are there any changes you want done to your will?" Peter asked Alfred. The two of them were walking down the side of the house to the gate.

Alfred kept his head firm. If he was surprised he didn't show it, and if he had been expecting that question, that was even harder to tell. "You think I should?" he said calmly.

"Hmmm. I don't know what you are thinking, Alfred."

"What do you mean?"

"Let's say I have a gut feeling that you aren't entirely comfortable with it."

"I'm not. How can I leave out my only child from all my life's hard work?"

Peter smiled at him. "I was right."

"Hello there, what a lovely morning to go for a walk," Pastor McIntosh said, walking up to the gate to meet them.

"Indeed it is, Pastor, we should just continue to walk. This is Peter Bradley, my barrister...I don't think you two have met," Alfred said.

"No we haven't. It's a pleasure, sir," Pastor McIntosh said, extending his hand.

"Glad to meet you, too, Pastor."

"Let's walk and talk as if we are back into our youthful days," Alfred grinned.

Peter and Pastor McIntosh agreed.

A hand parted the curtain of the house. A pair of eyes surveyed the gate. The three men walked away from it. Anita had never seen all three men together. Now that she had, a barrage of ideas floated in her head. She attempted to compare them, excluding his father of course. What she was examining was the potential for a kind of relationship with either of them. A question popped in her head: which one would you chose if there was a choice?

"Are you going out, Mother?" Andrew asked, coming up behind her.

Anita spun around. "Ohhh, no I...at least not yet."

"Can we talk?"

"Talk? Certainly. Is something wrong?"

"I-I-I..."

"Go on." Anita suspected what was coming. She felt her knees wobbled a bit. A burning sensation gripped the walls of her stomach. The sensation sent her back to doomsday—the day Jerome died; the feelings were similar. Those feelings returned despite the number of years that had passed. Anita sat on a chair nearby to regain her strength, attempting at all costs not to show her weakness. "Sit and let's talk."

"...Am...I've decided to go...." Tears were building up in his eyes. They became glossy. Anita reached out for him and they hugged each another.

"I know, son. It's for your father remember?" Anita said. "I'll be fine. You don't have to worry about me. I'll be alright."

"I have to do it. Slaves are suffering too much," he said between tears.

Anita felt a drop on her hand. It sent cold shivers over her body. Those were Jerome's tears; she was holding his own flesh and blood. Even though Anita thought she had gotten over Jerome, the bond would always be there. Andrew must do whatever he believed he had to do.

"I know of their plight. You go on, my son..."

"Where is he going?" Lynda asked. They turned to see her standing in the doorway hand akimbo. Lynda acted like she had heard a joke. The tone of her voice didn't have any seriousness about it.

"Andrew is going to Kingston, Mom."

"When? Why?"

"I'll be leaving tomorrow," he said softly. "I want to enter politics."

"C'mon, politics, you don't enter politics like that," Lynda said, pretty sure he was joking.

"I'll probably get into college first then move up from there."

"So you are serious?"

"I'm serious."

Anita watched her mother's reaction closely. She could easily see Lynda didn't approve of it. But then, Lynda and Alfred never approved of anything he did. Anita stood proud of her son. He had the guts to pursue a dream his father couldn't have done.

"How will you manage? Tell me this is a joke?" Lynda walked around the room in a semi-circle and came back to stand in front of him. Andrew wasn't in a military drill, yet the scrutinizing eyes of his grandmother placed him in the category of a new recruit on his first day on the inspection field.

"Grandma, this isn't a joke. My bags are already packed. All I need is a good horse."

"Hmmm. Just like..."

"Like Mom..." Anita interrupted. She knew what the next word would have been.

"Never mind. Does your grandfather know about this?"

"No, Grandma. I'll tell him today."

"Just like that? Do you know what the world is like out there?" she asked, walking around him again. "You have no money, no one in Kingston, but you are going there."

"The Baptist Church has hostels. I'll stay there until I can get a job."

"Oh. Do you know anyone in the Baptist Church?"

"I have a letter from Pastor McIntosh."

Anita watched her reaction again.

"I see. That's why you've been going to church nowadays. Did you put him up to this, Anita?"

Anita tried to control her anger. She did it well. "No, Mother. He mentioned it sometime ago. I never knew it would be so soon."

Lynda believed her. "Okay, Andrew, why not wait at least another week until we can help to make some arrangements for you. We could take you into Kingston."

Anita exchanged glances with her son. Andrew looked at them, wondering what he should do.

"Mom?"

"It's up to you, Andrew. I wouldn't mind going with you. I would have peace of mind because I would know where you are," she said, smiling and clutching his shoulder. She was anticipating a positive response from him. Lynda was smiling, one of those rare times when Andrew thought he truly had a grandmother.

"Okay, I'll leave next week."

The sun blazed down on Yardley Chase at the approach of midday. The heat was unbearable. It was a miracle that those who toiled in the field didn't faint or get sunstroke. The clouds had vacated the sky, giving the sun an all-clear sign to spread its rays where it wished. It took advantage of that.

The intense heat made John Stewart uncomfortable in his clothes. He could feel sweat trickling down his spine, as the sun seemed to be melting some of the excess fat from his hefty body. John wasn't working hard like the laborers; he was overseeing in the tobacco field. But standing in the sun alone was enough to make him sweat, although he wasn't exerting any energy. Probably he should go home at lunchtime to fix himself a hot meal. The sandwiches he had taken would be all soggy.

At midday, John mounted his horse for home. Something was troubling him very badly. John knew it but hated to admit anything. What he saw before his eyes sent him into a fit. He was raving mad; his appetite left him and so did his interest in work for the rest of the afternoon.

Peter and Anita were walking ahead of him. He tried to slow down his horse in order to trail them. Too late! Anita heard the heavy thud of the horse's hooves. She looked around to see John pulling up a few yards behind them.

"Hey there! Where are you charging to at this time of day? Going home for lunch?" Anita asked him.

"As a matter of fact I am," John said, without any expression on his face.

"It's pretty hot out there, John," Anita said, smiling at him.

"Oh boy, it's a miserable day," he retorted, trying very hard to conceal his anger.

"Don't worry, this heat should bring some rain," Peter said.

"I hope so. Anyway, I have to move on. I'll be seeing you."

"Bye, John," Anita said.

"John has truly been a loyal worker."

"He is very reliable. Poor John."

"Why did you say that?" Peter asked, turning to look at Anita.

"He was crazy about me some years ago."

"Hmm. As a matter of fact, I believe he hasn't changed his mind."

"What?" Anita exclaimed, stopping under a tree to get some shade.

"You haven't noticed how he looks at you. Even the blind could see his mannerism when you're around. Furthermore, that glow on his face whenever you say something to him tells a thousand words."

"You've been examining him."

"I have to do that."

"Who says so?"

"I have to examine from now on to ensure that the woman I think I'm falling in love with isn't interested in anyone else," Peter said, looking away in the direction of Lover's Leap.

Anita hesitated before looking into that direction, too. "That was quick."

"I knew from the last time I came."

"Why didn't you tell me then?"

"Jerome. He was in your thoughts, you thrive on his memory. I believe he's gone from your life at last."

"He is..."

"And..."

"I'm taking it one day at a time, Peter. I need to do that," she said, looking into his eyes, searching his face for something she wasn't even certain about at this time.

"Are you saying you aren't interested in me?"

"No, I'm not saying that, Peter. You are a very nice man. I couldn't deserve better. Let's take it as slowly as possible. Andrew is going away. It's a little confusing for me at this time."

"Andrew? Where to?"

"Kingston. He wants to go into politics to fight for the betterment of former slaves."

"Does he talk about his father?"

"He does that almost every day. Andrew believes he has to do it for him because he couldn't have done it."

"How do you feel about that?" Peter asked, taking her hand into his.

"I support him wholeheartedly. If he wants to go into politics, that's fine with me. Jerome was passionate about freedom. He was looking forward to being a free man."

"And for the day when the two of you could be together." Peter wished he could have taken back that comment. Nevertheless, it could give him some clue about what was going through Anita's beautiful head at this time.

"Yes, Peter. Jerome was looking forward to that."

"And you..."

"I won't lie to you. It was the only dream I had in this life," she said, without a hint of any apology.

"I'm wondering if you have truly got over Jerome, although you say you have," Peter said, scratching his chin.

Anita looked at Peter long and hard.

CHAPTER 5

An uneventful week crept by in Yardley Chase. Peter had returned to Black River four days ago. For Lynda, it was a mission accomplished, she thought. Alfred hadn't been well, staying indoors most of the time.

John covered most of Alfred's chores. He lingered around the house quite often to seize any opportunity he had to talk with Anita. Fortunately, he did that on a few occasions. At least it made him feel better. If that was the only short-term reward, so be it. John was elated Peter had gone. Maybe he wouldn't be back in a long, long time, much to his delight.

Anita told John of Andrew's impending departure on Sunday morning. He appeared pleasantly surprised. John wondered whether it would be a blessing or a curse. Andrew would leave tomorrow—Monday morning. He would visit church before he embarked on his mission.

The little stone-built church was perched on a knoll only a few yards from the road. Its white steeple stretched up into the sky, perhaps as a reminder to its members that Heaven was beyond the blue. Since it was constructed, the church had become the center of all community activities. It had become the lifeblood of Yardley Chase. It was all things to all people.

Lynda decided she would attend church today. Lynda, her daughter, and grandson walked up the hill to the church, where a crowd had already gathered outside. People were busily talking to one another. The subject being discussed seemed to have everyone's interest—even Pastor McIntosh.

They came in time to hear the pastor telling them, "Everything will be alright. God is in charge."

"What's that all about?" Lynda asked him, after the crowd began to scatter.

"Some violence is happening in St. James, Kingston and St. Thomas..."

"What may I ask?" Lynda said, cutting into his statement. Anita became curious, as well as Andrew.

"I understand a deacon...Paul something, is planning to organize protests over the conditions that former slaves have to work under. I'm afraid that could become ugly. Up to four days ago, no one was hurt. We're praying that it will remain like that."

"What's the Governor doing about it?"

"He has troops in the potential trouble spots, my dear. I hear most of the trouble is around Morant Bay, Stoney Gut areas." A few people had come back to listen to what the pastor was saying.

"You know Andrew leaves for Kingston tomorrow," Anita said.

"I know."

"Should he?" Lynda asked.

Pastor McIntosh looked at Andrew admiringly. "You know what. If you want, I can travel to Kingston with you. I think that would be advisable. I have some business there, too. I know how to get around, I'd take him straight to the church there."

"Oh! How wonderful!" Lynda blurted out.

"That's the best news I can get right now," Anita said, a radiant smile gripping her face.

"Thanks, Pastor. I don't know how to thank you," Andrew said, shaking his hand. "How will the church do without you?"

"Don't worry, the deacons will take care. Who're the people going with you?"

"Grandma, Mom, Jerry and Simon," Andrew replied.

"That sounds like a good team. Let's get the service going and afterward we can start getting our things together."

Pastor McIntosh was at his best during services. He lashed out against the impoverished state of the country's former slaves, citing references to Jesus' ministry on earth healing the sick and tending to the poor. However, he was cautious in noting that civil unrest wasn't the answer, but rather the coming together of everyone for the common good. Jesus, he said, should be the island's guide in any goals or policies the colonial government might pursue.

Lynda was very attentive during the services. She could understand some of his arguments. She wished some plantation owners were like Alfred, who tried his best to ensure his laborers got the appropriate treatment.

Andrew liked the sermon. Pastor McIntosh could become a trusted politician. His voice came across with force and authority. Furthermore, he was knowledgeable to the happenings in Kingston and the rural areas. It was a pity the Pastor McIntosh was far from Kingston. He could have been a strong voice to bring the plight of former slaves to the forefront of issues to be dealt in the House of Assembly.

Anita was the one who was the most attentive. Her eyes never left Pastor McIntosh as he gyrated around the pulpit, stomping his feet, clenching his fist to hammer home a point. His voice echoed with emotion as he emptied his mind of all the troubling and uneasiness that had been building up there for some time. Pastor McIntosh was touching on a very passionate subject. From all indications, the welfare of the poor was foremost on his mind. The recent civil unrest acted as a catalyst for this sermon.

During Pastor McIntosh's spectacular performance, Anita thought he looked at her occasionally. It was difficult to tell. She and her family were near the front. The pastor would have to look in their direction in order to maintain eye contact with the entire room of about fifty people. The more she looked at him, the more she was becoming impressed.

Pastor McIntosh appeared to command a lot of respect and admiration from his members, particularly a young woman Anita observed sitting in the front row. They were all very attentive. It was the first time Anita had seen her at church.

Indeed, if this was her first visit, certainly she must be impressed. Because Anita was sitting to the side of her, the seemingly permanent smile on her face must mean something. Who was this young woman? What troubled Anita even more was her astounding beauty.

Alfred wanted to tell Lynda to stay with him, rather than taking that long journey into Kingston. Anita, maybe John, Jerry and Solomon should be able to take care of everything. Alfred hadn't been feeling well since mid-week. He said nothing to Lynda about it but he wished he had done that before.

Early Sunday morning, Alfred felt like he had passed out for a few minutes. He had been having such a difficult time sleeping that he went into the kitchen for some water. Alfred was sitting in a chair listening to the nocturnal sounds coming from outside. The next moment he found himself trying to rise from the floor. He couldn't move. The sounds coming from his mouth were garbled. Alfred remained there for about forty-five minutes before he could get up. He went back to bed. By the time he woke up they had all gone to church. Had he been up, perhaps he would have gone to church, too.

Alfred decided he must make peace with his only grandson before his departure. In so doing, Alfred realized that he would also be making a truce with his daughter.

"Are you alright, Alfred?" John asked, as he walked up to him sitting under the star apple tree at the former Hell House.

"Oh! You frightened me. I didn't hear you walk up," Alfred said feebly.

"Your mind must be out of this world. Worried about the price for sugar?"

"No, no, that's the least right now," he assured him.

"What are you worried about?"

"Nothing in particular. I was only reflecting on those horrible nights slaves must have had out here years ago."

"You know they deserve the punishment," John said soberly.

"In my old age, I harbor doubts about that, John. The memories are haunting me. The memories sicken me; they've become a nightmare," he said scornfully.

"Don't tell me you are converting."

"It's time I do."

"Hmm, you should've gone to church today like the others."

"I woke up late."

"You were thinking of going?" John asked, sitting beside him, brushing back his hair from his face.

"I could have. I wanted to go with Andrew. You know he leaves tomorrow."

"I heard talk about that. How's he going?"

"As a matter of fact, I was thinking of asking you to accompany Anita, Jerry and Simon. Lynda's going but I want to ask her to stay."

"I would be happy to go. You know that." He grinned. "Sometimes a man needs a break from Yardley Chase."

"If I could take the journey I would, too."

"Well, sir, I'm ready to go if you want me to."

"I want you to go, John."

Lynda didn't hang around after church was over. However, her daughter had a good reason to—she wanted to find out more about this mystery woman. Andrew wanted to go home to prepare for his journey tomorrow, and left his mother at church.

Anita was happy to be alone. She remained inside the church after Lynda and Andrew had gone. It was a smart thing to do because as soon as the crowd started to disappear, Pastor McIntosh came over to her. The mystery woman disappeared quickly. One moment Anita saw her talking to the pastor, the next minute she was nowhere to be seen.

"The others left?" Pastor McIntosh asked Anita.

"Yes. They wanted to get everything ready for tomorrow. I'm more than ready. I was about leaving, too." She smiled, a little disappointment in her voice.

"You sound as if you are missing him already. Are you alright?"

"I have to admit I'm sad to see him go, but he must fulfil this desire."

"On the other hand, I think you've a young son that will one day make you feel proud."

"I think so, too." Anita wished she could find a way of determining who was that young woman at church.

"Andrew is a very articulate and smart young man who we'll be hearing a lot about in years to come."

"Hmmm. Jerome would've been proud."

"Certainly. I guess at this time thoughts of him come flowing back to you," he said solemnly.

"They do, although not in any hurtful way," Anita said, looking at him admiringly, "time has healed the wounds. I know I have to move on."

"That's good, Anita. You've surely come a long way."

Anita wished he could just hold her at that moment. That would never happen. She knew it; there would be another time and place for that opportunity, she thought with a smile.

On their way home, Lynda thought she would make use of this moment to make up for lost time and opportunities with Andrew. The eastern sky was a flurry of black moving dots. She watched the crows circling nearby. *What carrion was attracting them so much?* she wondered.

"They are quite busy over there," she said, pointing in that direction.

"They're smelling something," Andrew said.

"I would imagine you'll also be a busy young man in the coming weeks," Lynda said, looking around at him.

"Yes, Grandma. It will be very much different from what goes on at Yardley Chase."

"Hmm. Yardley Chase, no more chasing of slaves or former slaves around the yard; they are free yet remain in shackles?"

"That's right. They deserve better. Would you agree?"

"Oh definitely! You deserve better, too, Andrew, and Alfred and I are truly sorry that we've been ignoring you all these years."

Andrew looked at his grandmother, expressionless. "Is this something the two of you have been discussing?"

"We have, Andrew. We've erred. We couldn't accept your father but that doesn't mean we shouldn't have accepted you.

I can assure you that we have now," Lynda said, her voice pleading as if she was begging pardon. "It's long overdue."

"We all make mistakes. It's good when we can recognize them, acknowledging our shortcomings before it's too late. Thank God I haven't built up any kind of resentment toward both of you over the years. I had a good roof over my head, more than enough to eat, good clothes to wear. Thanks to both of you. I wanted parental care, and that I got that from my mother in immeasurable proportions."

"Anita is a good woman. We have had our disagreements but we know she has done well with you. You're our only grandchild. Right now, Andrew, I can tell you we are proud of you. Alfred wants me to go with you to Kingston to ensure that you're taken care of in all your needs. We have pledged to do that, maybe the least we can do at this time. It's not a way of making up the lost years. I think it's our duty.

"Thank you, Grandma."

Lynda stopped in the middle of the walk, turned around, and hugged her grandson. She tried to remember when she ever did something like that. It must have been the first time.

Andrew was pleasantly surprised. What more appropriate could he do at this time than hug her, too? It was a comfortable feeling because he would be leaving Yardley Chase on good terms, plus he was going with the support of his rich grandparents.

They walked up to the house where John and Alfred were sitting under the tree at Hell House.

"Where's Anita?" Alfred asked.

"She stayed back a few minutes to talk with the pastor," Lynda replied.

John's heart skipped a beat before returning to its normal rate. He had more reasons for being suspicious.

"By the way," Lynda continued, "Pastor McIntosh has offered to accompany us to Kingston. There have been some disturbances going on in the east. He thought it would be wise to take us to the Baptist Mission there. He knows many people in the city."

"Oh, that sounds great. I was saying to John here that you should stay and let him go with the others."

"Me, stay? Why? Are you alright?"

"That's something I have to talk to you about. John is willing to go. He would be an asset to this trip because of his traveling experience," Alfred said, sitting upright in his seat.

"What about Pastor McIntosh?" Andrew asked.

"He can go if he wants to. He has good contacts there?" Alfred said.

"Uh I-I think that would be fine with me," John mumbled.

"Good! Then you all have a date without me," Lynda said, somewhat disappointed, but eager to hear from Alfred the reason for discouraging her not to go.

"I'm not feeling that great these last few days, Lynda. I need you around," he told her as soon as Andrew and John had left.

"Is there something I should know?"

"Not really. Sometimes I'm very exhausted," he said, wondering if he should tell her what happened to him this morning.

"You may need to take it easy. All right, I understand. You need to get some rest. I'll fill in for you wherever possible."

"Does Andrew really want to go?"

"He wants to go. I can see why. We had a good talk on the way here. I tried to tell him how much we're sorry for ignoring him. Thank God he's not bitter."

"I'm glad, too. I'll give Anita more than enough money to pay his expenses for the next two years."

"That's rather generous. I know he'll appreciate it."

"We're doing what we should've been doing from day one. Anita, I suspect, is taking a liking to Pastor," Alfred said.

"Hmm. I've been observing that myself."

"What about Peter?"

"I didn't get to discuss any detail with him. I can see he's impressed with her."

"Well, Peter may have competition. Of late, Anita is at church every Sunday, and sometimes during mid-week."

"Let's say, a new day is dawning for our daughter," Lynda said, smiling. She looked into her husband's eyes, remembering the good times they had in the past.

Alfred clasped his hand over hers. "I'm glad things are looking better for her."

Leonora Simmonds' first week in Jamaica had gotten off to a good start. She and her father, Dr. Gladstone Simmonds, had arrived from England last week to begin practice in the southern part of St. Elizabeth. His area covered some fifteen miles to the east, ten miles north another eighteen miles west. Their office was located between the districts of Yardley Chase and Top Hill.

Lenora was a devoted Christian. The day after she arrived she started to search for a church. Their neighbor recommended the one at Yardley Chase. It was Baptist, and the nearest Anglican Church was in Southfield, two miles away. However, the Baptist church wasn't that far from Leonora. She would visit the Anglican Church soon but for the time being would visit the Baptist.

Dr. Simmonds watched his daughter as she came up the steps of their house. He had a hard day unpacking. About an hour ago, he sat down on the porch for an afternoon sun bath. It wasn't that hot compared with yesterday; the massive clouds hovering above and blotted out the sun's rays. A few rays managed to peep through the cotton white clouds at times. However, they didn't stay long because the clouds seemed to be spreading their tentacles to cover whatever blue patches were visible.

The doctor looked pale in this tropical climate. His graying hair made him look older than his fifty-five years, although his muscular frame added to his appearance as a person who was constantly busy. He soared to nearly six feet, whereas his daughter was a mere five feet 4 inches. Leonora inherited that from her mother, Gloria, who died ten years ago. Lenora was only fifteen.

A stunningly beautiful young woman, Leonora also looked pale like her father. The English winters had absorbed any little sunburn she might have gotten over the years. The Jamaican climate could soon change all of that. Leonora's long red hair rested on her shoulders, blending nicely with her conical face.

Dr. Simmonds wanted to go to church with her but chores at home made it almost impossible. He, too, was deeply religious, always looking forward to the services and fellowshipping. He could see the broad smile on his daughter's face as she came closer. She had found a comfortable place to worship.

"How was it?" he asked her anxiously.

"Great, Dad! It was great...nice people, a good sermon. It's also pretty near. I came back with the Bennetts," she said, pointing to their neighbor up the road.

"I'm delighted to hear that. I'll go with you next Sunday."

"Pastor McIntosh has only been here two years."

"Oh! The pastor is fairly new."

"I had expected to see an elderly man."

"He isn't?"

"He's young, maybe around forty," she smiled.

"Hmmm, that sounds interesting."

"He's very friendly, very articulate. The people are quite friendly, too. I can hardly wait to go back next week."

"I'm looking forward to going."

"At least we've something to look forward to next Sunday," Leonora said, images of Pastor McIntosh flashing across her mind.

At Jack's Place, Alfred waited until supper was over before making his move. He walked up the stairs feebly heading straight for Andrew's room. The door was opened; he knocked before he stepped in. Anita was there, too. Both heads turned to see their visitor. It was Alfred's house, yet this room wasn't one that he often visited. Anita and Andrew expected something unusual to happen here this evening.

"We have to talk, son," he said, sitting down in a chair beside the bed.

The room was silent, nobody said anything.

"The time has come for me to make peace with my only daughter, my grandson, too," he said, trembling in his voice.

Anita walked over to her father and hugged him while he remained seated. Andrew did the same. Soon after, the sobs came, and an emotional outburst filled the whole room. Lynda, who was coming up the stairs, heard everything. She rushed into the room quickly. Words wouldn't make sense at this time. The tears, the hugs, spoke louder than words. Anita poured out her years of sadness. Alfred emptied himself of all the angry feelings he had, while Lynda soothed her troubles with the exchange of pleasantries between father and daughter. Andrew was the bond between all of them. The acceptance of his departure tomorrow brought home the message that it was time this "war" was over.

It was dark outside. Inside, the faint light from the lone lamp shone on their faces, revealing streaks of tears crawling down faces; eyelids were swollen from the strain brought on the eyes. It was a good two minutes before anything was said. Anita was on her knees, her head in her father's lap. Andrew was holding onto his mother. Lynda stretched out both hands to embrace husband and daughter.

"Heavenly Father, I thank you for this moment," Anita said under her breath. "It couldn't have been possible without you."

"Thank you, Jesus," Andrew said.

"Amen," Lynda said.

"I thank you, too, Father God," Alfred mumbled. "Forgive us for what we have done to them over the years. We're truly sorry. Guide my grandson on his journey, his desire to make this country a better place for all. I'm not much of a praying person but this I ask of you, Father. Bless him and be with him always in Jesus' name, Amen."

It was the first time Andrew and Anita heard Alfred using the word grandson. They were convinced his gesture was genuine. They all got up from the floor and sat on the bed.

"We've pledged to give you all the assistance we can," Alfred said to Andrew, turning to address him. "You won't be in need of anything. We'll pay your living expenses for two years. At the end of that time, more help will be forthcoming for as long as you need it. You're my only grandchild."

"Thank you, Grandpa."

"Dad, this is so nice of you."

"I'm getting old. This is the least I can do for you, Andrew. In a sense, maybe I'm trying to make up for all those years. I want to be honest. I couldn't accept your father then but now things are different. Lynda and I have seen our error; we feel it's best to put all that behind us in order to move on with our lives. Our duty now is to you, our only grandchild."

Anita reached out and hugged her parents. Indeed, the war with them was over; the other was to get over Jerome once and for all. "Thank you. Thank you, Dad...it feels good to be accepted again."

Andrew sat in bed practically all night, staring at the dark ceiling. The day's developments were too much to overlook. Imagine, tomorrow he would ride away from Yardley Chase and beautiful Lover's Leap. He would leave his mother behind to live on her memories and to forge a new and meaningful relationship with her parents. Andrew would also leave a trail of hopelessness for hundreds of former slaves who looked for each day to come with something better—renewed hope.

Andrew felt guilty. Nevertheless, the only thing he could lean on for support was the possibility that his departure could bring some results in the future. That might be only a dream; Andrew intended to make it a reality.

On the other hand, since the past month Andrew had watched his mother's life turning for the better. What happened a few hours ago in his room bore testimony to that.

Peter was interested in his mother. Andrew was reluctant to believe that at first. He almost bumped into them while they had been hugging one night. That was the evidence. Furthermore, a sensitive Andrew picked up a magnetic field between Pastor McIntosh and his mother. He suspected the pastor might not be aware of it, or he was but was ignoring it.

Had his mother finally got over the dad he never knew? Undoubtedly, she had tried hard not to; she loved him with such passion that Andrew was afraid Anita would never love again. The past month told him she could, if she found the right person.

Andrew's thoughts raced to John. Anita had told him of

John's hatred for Jerome, and his relentless efforts to destroy their relationship in order to win her love. Did he still have thoughts about her? Andrew could not answer that question. Neither could he provide an answer to his mother's thoughts on Peter or the pastor. He could ask her, knowing the kind of relationship he had with Anita, and she would give him an answer. It wouldn't be a wise idea to ask that question right now, he concluded. One thing Andrew knew, though: a battle was shaping up, a battle for his mother.

CHAPTER 6

Teddy's second crow brought his master to his feet. The familiar early morning sound penetrated the atmosphere like a buckshot. Teddy belted it out as if it was his last one.

Andrew parted the window and looked outside. It was dark except for a glare along the horizon in the direction of Lover's Leap. A new day was being born in the life of Andrew. In a few hours, he would ride toward the rising sun and into a region he didn't know much about. He spent the next few moments thinking about his past life at Jack's Place, moreso the episode last night with his grandparents. Suddenly, years of isolation had culminated in one big reunion. At least he was leaving on good terms.

Andrew got dressed slowly envisaging what life would be in the next few weeks without his dear mother, without Yardley Chase. From all indications, he would be in good hands; the church would be his refuge and strength, and its master, Jesus Christ, would guide his footsteps.

There were some rumblings at the back of the house near the stable. Andrew crossed the room to the other window to see what was happening. John was there with the horses and buggy. He could see two other people lurking in the shadows; he soon recognized them as Jerry and Simon who were making trips from the stable.

John! Pastor McIntosh! If the battle for his mother was on, as he suspected, this journey would be very, very, interesting. He would only know about the first leg of the journey. He hoped everything would go smoothly, doubting the pastor had even a slight hint of his mother's soft spot for him. If there was going to be an aggressor, it had to be John.

Andrew finished dressing; he stepped out into the cool morning air. Its freshness was a reminder that it was a brand new day for him, a new day for Yardley Chase. Teddy was in the yard to meet him. The rooster got more than the usual amount of corn, as a special treat.

"This is your bonus," Andrew said, taking him up. "You've been a good pet. But don't worry, you'll be taken care of until I pass through for a visit. I hope no one eats you." He grinned. Teddy clucked away looking down at the faintly visible corn on the ground.

"I promise you he'll be fine. I'll make sure no one eats him," John said, coming up behind Andrew.

"I know he'll be in good hands. I'm missing him already."

"When you leave here this morning, you're going on your own. You're telling the world you're a grown man. This pet here is a reminder of where you're coming from. You're leaving him because you're no longer a child," John said, watching the rooster searching in the dark for the grains of corn.

"Smart words, John. That's something to think about."

"You'll leave your mom. She won't be around to advise you or to provide any help you may need. You'll be on your own."

"She's a good mom."

"The best."

"You mean that?"

"I mean it, son. She has tried very hard with you, despite the challenges."

"I can see you never stopped admiring her, John."

John turned away without answering. "Time to go, son, time to go."

They went to the house to find everyone, including Pastor McIntosh, assembled in the kitchen. The smell of coffee and fresh bread filled the air. Grace was said, and they started sipping and munching in silence, except the crunching sound from their mouths.

Dawn was disappearing by the time they were finished. Jerry, John, and Simon proceeded to the buggy while Andrew bade farewell. Andrew hugged his grandparents not wanting to let go. He withdrew reluctantly with tears in his eyes.

"Remember we're here. Get a message or letter to us if you need help. We'll be there. God be with you, son, please keep in touch," Alfred said, patting him on his shoulder.

"You'll do well. This country will hear about you someday. My instinct tells me everything will turn out fine. God be with you," Lynda said.

"Thanks, I'll remember your words. You take care of yourselves. I'll keep you informed on what's happening. God bless."

"You'll do great, son," Pastor McIntosh said.

A teary-eyed Anita watched without saying anything. If she had attempted to say something, she knew the tears would flow down her cheeks.

Andrew made one final hug. This time he went over to embrace the two maids who were looking on. Alfred and Lynda watched as everyone boarded the buggy. John gave the signal. The horses bolted through the gate as if they had seen a green pasture. Alfred and Lynda were relieved because peace of mind had finally come to Jack's Place. In a sense, Andrew's father was the one who started the "war." His illegitimate son was the one who ended it.

Black River was one busy port town. The town was perched on the edge of the rugged coastline that stretched away into the distant. The breeze from the sea caressed the buildings constantly, providing relief from the intense heat that blanketed the town daily.

The main town in the parish had quite a few buildings along its main street. One of them was Peter Bradley's office.

The back of his office faced the sea. Each time the waves rolled onto the shore, the wind accompanying it ruffled some of the papers on his desk. Some were blown to the floor making his office one big mess. Peter made no move to retrieve the papers; he was too busy thinking about the woman of his dreams.

It was past midday. He had done nothing since morning. Every time he started to do something, Anita's smiling face stopped him. It wasn't like that before he went to Yardley Chase. However, that one visit must have cast a spell on him. He wished she was in town, or lived nearby. That would have made things much better.

Peter was convinced he had to pay another visit soon. Anita was lonely and vulnerable now that she had been getting over Jerome. Peter could consider himself a lucky man if Anita would share even a small portion of the love she had for Jerome. Time had been healing her wounds. Perhaps it was a matter of time before she started showing more interest, Peter thought. He would have to visit more often.

Thirty miles away in the Spur Tree Hills, Anita, her son, and the rest of the group had their first stop since they had started early that morning. Had Peter known that two potential competitors were with Anita, he would have closed his office to call it a day. The other option would be to ride up to Yardley Chase to see her.

They sat under a tree enjoying the cool wind blowing across the mountain range. Anita's thoughts weren't on Peter. Her thoughts were on the mystery woman she had seen at church.

"How much would it cost to hear what's on your mind? Or is the answer in there already? Andrew?" Pastor McIntosh said, coming up beside Anita. Andrew and the two boys were scouting the area. John was pretty near; he cleared his ear to pick up the conversation.

"I can't deny that, Pastor. I'm missing him already and he's here. I guess I have to get used to his absence."

"That's a wise approach. You won't have that true experience until you return to Yardley Chase to find he's not around."

"You're right. I'm already beginning to take comfort in the fact that he's doing this because of his father's desire for freedom. When I say freedom I mean complete freedom, economic and social."

Pastor McIntosh stooped down on the grass beside her. "I can see how much you loved Jerome. No wonder you adore Andrew. That's all that's left of him physically. I have every confidence that Andrew won't disappoint any of us."

John had been finding the conversation interesting, so far. He pretended he was watching the horses feed on the rich mound of grass beside him.

"Pastor, you're such a considerate man. I've met no one like you. I came to you with my troubled and sinful self, you're always there...to encourage to help me in any way you can," she said, smiling and nodding her head at the same time.

"That's what I've been called to do by a God who recognizes one's desire to serve."

"Do you enjoy doing what you are doing?" Anita asked earnestly.

"Of course I do."

"I often wonder how you do it. You don't have a family."

"By the grace of God, I believe."

"Can I ask you a personal question?" Anita asked, suspecting she might be going into forbidden territory.

"Shoot. I don't mind. In the ministry, one has to be open in order to deal with some of the problems facing others."

"I don't mean to intrude. Don't you get lonely sometimes?" Anita kept her focus on him because she wanted to see his reaction. There was none. The question didn't ring any alarms.

"Anita, I'm as human as you are. I do get lonely sometimes; however, let's say my work keeps me very busy that I don't have time to think about loneliness."

"Hmmm, a smart way to survive."

"I guess you could say that."

"Will you ever get married and settle down with a family?" Anita asked, remembering Leonora at that moment.

"It could happen. I must emphasize, though, that I don't see that happening anytime soon."

"Why?" she asked, a ring of curiosity in her voice.

"I'm pretty new around here; furthermore, I don't know how long I'll be around."

"What do you mean?" Anita was even more curious.

"One of the reasons I'm going to Kingston is to get a better idea of what's going on there. The Baptist Mission has been coming under a lot of pressure to deal with some of the problems since emancipation. I've a feeling my presence may be needed in Kingston some time in the near future."

Anita's heart raced a little faster. She didn't like what she was hearing. The prospect was looming that she could be walking a very lonely road in the near future. Andrew was going and the person, who has been helping to change her outlook on life, might soon be going, too. She thought of Jerome for a few seconds.

"That would be sad, Pastor, because many people look up to you for guidance, myself included."

"I may be stuck here for the rest of my life for all I care. In life, one never knows. I have to follow where the Spirit leads me; at the same time, I wouldn't worry about that."

"It is nice to hear you say that." A rather pleasant smile came across her face.

A few feet away, the partially hidden figure of John was smiling, too. He had heard what Pastor McIntosh said about the possibility of leaving Yardley Chase. That would be a great gift for John. Anita's apparent obsession with the pastor would be hurt by his departure. She would have no one to lean on for support—except John, of course. John forgot to include Peter because he wasn't certain what was going on with him. Those questions from Anita were enough to convince John that she was very much interested in Pastor McIntosh.

Somehow, John told himself he had a duty to do his part in encouraging the pastor to pack and leave Yardley Chase as soon as possible. He laughed to himself because he knew it wouldn't be a difficult task.

After the break, they boarded the buggy and took the road to Kingston, once more. They would stay the night in Mandeville or Porus, depending on how exhausted they would be by nightfall.

Leonora Simmonds mounted the black stallion her father had bought for her, and rode to the Yardley Chase Baptist Church. She told her father she was going for a ride but had no doubts about where she was heading. Leonora wanted to see Pastor McIntosh again—and very badly. She dreamt about him last night and had a challenging time ridding her mind of his smiling face. As far as she was concerned, she desired to have some sort of counseling from him, if what Leonora had up her sleeve could be called anything near that.

The day was hot and miserable. It was hard to imagine that there were heavy showers a few days ago. The usual wind from Lover's Leap wasn't blowing today. The vegetation withered from the heat, leaving half-dead leaves and near dry grass. The feet of the stallion pounded against the dusty trail, sending loose dirt on top of the already struggling weeds and small trees along the side of the road. They had started to take on the color of the soil in that section of the island. The soil in those parts was different from other areas of the island. Local residents described it as red.

Leonora rode to the pastor's manse. She slid from the saddle with the agility of a trained horseman. She quickly walked up to the front door, knocked about six times, but there was no answer.

"Pastor is nat dere," said a voice.

Startled by the sudden utterance from out of nowhere, Leonora turned in the direction of the voice.

"Oh! Oh! hi...he's not in?"

"No, missus." A smiling Sally beamed at her. "Him nat in t'day."

"I was hoping to see him. Do you know what time he'll be back?"

Sally was coming to plant some flowers around the manse when the knocking drew her attention. She knew the pastor accompanied Andrew to Kingston. "In another week, missus."

"One week!" she exclaimed. "Do you mean he's away?"

"Yes'um."

"Where did he go?" Leonora asked, finding it difficult to believe her story.

"Gone to Kingston, missus, an' a don't t'ink he's coming back till Mondi."

"You mean on Monday?" she asked, trying to make sense of what she had said.

Sally nodded.

"A whole week is long to me. Are you sure about that because I don't want to come out here again and he's not here."

"He an' Miss Anita an' har son, mi bredda an' Pastor all gone together."

"Who's Miss Anita?"

"Yuh don't know har? Yuh new aroun' here? Can' say I 'member seein' yuh, missus. Miss Anita live in dat big house ova dere. Yuh can see di big yard...see, jus' look between di trees," she said, pointing.

"Hmm, that's a huge house there."

"Yes, missus, de bigges' 'round here."

"Well, I guess I have to come back another time. Will they have church on Sunday?"

"Oh yes'um. Deacon wi help out wid di service."

"What's your name, I didn't remember to ask?" Leonora smiled for the first time.

"Sally."

"Okay, Sally, I'm sure I'll see you again."

"Walk good, missus, and I'll tell Pastor yuh stop by."

"Leonora is the name."

"Leo...nor...a. Leonora, right, missus," she said, giggling.

"That's right, Sally. I'll be seeing you soon."

"Bye, missus."

Sally watched her mounted the black stallion. From whence did this new face emerge? Why was she in such a hurry to see the pastor?

A few yards away at Jack's Place, the atmosphere was one of an uneasy calm. Anita and Andrew's absence was being felt—terribly. The day was so hot that Alfred and Lynda decided to stay indoors in the living room. Alfred was sipping some lemonade while Lynda was gazing out into the blue sky.

"You are missing them, too?" Alfred asked.

"I cannot deny that. Never thought it would've been like this." She looked at him, seeing the dreariness in his eyes.

"I'm learning in my old age what it means to really have an only child. No matter how things went in the past, maturity tells you it's not that difficult to forgive and forget."

"I share the same view, Alfred. I'm happy that we came to our senses before it's too late."

"Do you believe Anita has forgiven us?"

"I've no doubts about that. What I see in Anita is a woman waiting to be forgiven," she said, removing the hair from her face. "Sometimes I tend to believe that if we had forgiven her long ago it wouldn't have taken that long for her to get over Jerome."

"You may be right. My dear, it's never too late to learn." He smiled. "My fervent hope is to see her find a nice husband like Peter to settle down."

"I think his trip was worth it."

"Do think she suspects you may have been behind it?"

"I doubt that. I was hoping Peter wouldn't move too fast."

"If he did, my very sensitive daughter could have some suspicion."

"And I think she would've confronted me already. She hasn't done that, rest assured that she doesn't have a clue."

Alfred turned in his chair to place himself in a more comfortable position. "I'm a little puzzled though about Pastor McIntosh's decision to accompany them into Kingston."

"You are! I see no harm in that, although I hesitated at first."

"Why did you hesitate?"

"I thought about Peter, but then I trust Pastor McIntosh. I don't believe there's anything going on between them. Anita is seeking spiritual guidance, fortunately that is all she's getting."

"And John?" Alfred asked softly.

"If there's anything going on between them, John will be a stumbling block."

"Would it come as a surprise if I tell you John is still interested in her?"

"Hmmm, after all that rejection. What makes you think so?" Lynda asked.

"Anything you ask John to do regarding Anita he'll not turn you down. There's a message in that."

"Since you mentioned it, you're quite correct. Did he volunteer to go to Kingston?"

"No, I asked him. He was more than willing."

"I hope we don't get the return of an angry and disappointed John after that trip," Lynda mused.

About twenty-five miles away, in the village of Porus, everyone on the trip bedded down for the night. The weary and tired souls had their supper then went straight to bed. Anita was the only one who wasn't sleeping. She listened to her son's snore on a nearby bed in the hotel they were staying in. It brought back memories of a night she spent in Porus many years ago. They were on their way to Spanish Town to meet Lynda, who had just arrived from England. Jerome was on that trip. It was on a night like this when everyone had been sleeping that she sneaked out on one of her secret rendezvous with Jerome. There were many. Andrew was conceived on one of them, she suspected. A night like this wasn't one she could easily forget. To get rid of Jerome wasn't going to be easy, because he was involved in every facet of her life.

In the room next to Anita was a man whom she had grown to respect very much in the past few weeks. She had been struggling to forget Jerome. Undoubtedly, he had been helping her to do that knowingly and unknowingly. Anita had been sensing something else in the past few days. The respect she had for him had been growing into something else. She dismissed the idea at first. The few days she had with Peter were great. Peter was very interested in her, at least he told her he was. But as soon as Peter was gone, the pastor was the one who was constantly in her thoughts.

If the man next door wasn't a pastor, Anita knew she would be apt to repeat the same tactics she used with Jerome. A man of God was next door, a servant of God who brought cheer, hope; a man who made life meaningful to many people, including her. She couldn't slip into his room; she had too much respect for him to ever do that. At the same time, Anita was convinced that the pastor didn't have the slightest inclination that she was interested in him. It was something she would have to live with until he could see things the way she was doing now. This journey would be one of memories, she concluded. After recollecting events of the past, reflecting on the present, and examining the possibilities of the future, Anita pulled the sheet over her head and fell asleep smiling.

Directly below Anita, downstairs, John Stewart kept peering up into the dark ceiling. Anita was up there, he thought. John wished he had the answer for whatever was on Anita's mind. In addition, he hoped it would be something he would be able to take care of. That was a long shot. John knew that.

Pastor McIntosh woke up after midnight in time to hear words coming from his mouth. He became conscious so quickly that the sound of the last few words died in the silence of the room. The only word he remembered saying was "Leonora." *Strange*, he thought, while not even bothering to recall his dream.

The pastor was the first to get up next morning, at least that was what he thought. John was already outside grooming the horse when he stepped outside. John saw him coming and continued to do what he had been doing.

"I thought I'd be the first to rise," Pastor McIntosh told him.

"Hmmm, you're wrong, Pastor. I've been up early." John grinned.

"Couldn't sleep?"

"Sleep was alright. I'm usually an early riser. You didn't sleep well?"

"I slept very deep. I even had a nightmare."

"Huh that must've been something."

Anita waltzed toward them, her long skirt scraping the gravel and grass that were on the walkway. They both saw her coming.

"Huh, we seem to have a lot of early risers today," the pastor guessed.

"Good morning, gentlemen."

"Morning," John said abruptly.

"Good morning, you're up early," Pastor McIntosh said, searching her face for drowsiness and noting the bulging eyes. "You look rested."

"I cannot complain. Did you both have coffee?"

"I have," John said, a little abrupt.

"I'd do well with a cup."

"The innkeeper has a huge pot waiting."

"I could need more than one, I better go for it."

As soon as the pastor stepped off, John seized on the opportunity to talk.

"How have you been enjoying the trip?"

"Pretty good."

"It must be hard for you to see Andrew leaving," he said, brushing the mane of one of the horses.

"I'm getting over that. He's a grown man. He must do what he has to do."

"If you need someone to talk to you know I'm always here for you, Anita."

"I..."

Andrew bumped right into the dialogue. "John, how long have you been here?"

"From daybreak."

"Hmmm, you truly mean business. Did you get something to eat?

"Yeah. I'm alright."

"The others are eating. As soon as they're finished we can."

The lone bark of a dog broke the silence of the surroundings. A feeble crow from a rooster echoed across the main street. The wheels of the buggy parted soft mud leaving its mark, as it moved away from the inn to the east. The street was deserted. It was a misty morning in Porus, a regular occurrence in the mountainous village.

Anita saw the pastor shivering. She offered him an extra wool sweater she had around her arms.

"Thank you, my dear. For a moment I thought I was in Manchester, England, not Manchester, Jamaica."

"It's certainly cooler than Yardley Chase."

"For sure."

"Is Kingston very hot, Pastor?" Andrew asked.

"Hotter than Hell," he joked.

"That hot?" Andrew said, as if he believed him.

"Kingston is always hot. I don't want to frighten you but it must be even hotter with all that may be going on there."

"The politics, you mean?"

"Yes. That's what you're interested in?"

"Certainly, I want to know more about that young Baptist pastor who's now in the House of Assembly. I understand he's for the ex-slaves and he wants that nine pence a day wage increase."

"He's getting a following for that. Have you ever thought about the possibility of not making it into politics?"

Anita listened attentively to his answer. Andrew shrugged before answering.

"I'll make it...at all costs. It isn't a matter of making it, Pastor, it's a matter of doing what I have to do. It won't be easy but I guarantee you that I'll play my part in speaking and doing more for the oppressed."

"You sound like a politician already," John teased from up front, where he was holding the reins. Jerry and Simon listened in silence. They admired Andrew a lot because they knew he was on their side. The break from Yardley Chase was a relief; the cause made the journey even more meaningful for them.

"I have to start sounding like one or else no one will listen to me," Andrew shouted back, trying to drown out the clanging of wheels against stones and the thud of hooves against the road surface.

Anita looked at her son and she wanted to hug him. Her glance shifted from him to the pastor sitting next to Andrew. She wanted to hug him, too. Peter came to mind in the next moment; so was John with his invitation an hour ago. Jerome also slipped into the picture, and Anita stared ahead of her with a blank expression on her face.

Andrew would be out of her life soon. Anita had no doubts that companionship was going to be an important component of her life. She was going to get lonely. Although her parents would be there, the void that had been created since Jerome's departure would have to be filled. Andrew played an integral role in helping her not to see the need for any meaningful relationship. She would no longer see or talk with Andrew every day.

Peter Bradley had everything she could hope for. A profession, looks, and he could afford a decent lifestyle. She didn't want to assess the pastor because he was in a different category. He showed no interest in her romantically; however, he had characteristics that she had difficulty finding words to describe. Pastor McIntosh had an answer for everything. He was deeply spiritual, using the scriptures to explain all the intricacies of life and death. He lived on hope, worrying about nothing whatsoever. Imagine he didn't have a family, yet loneliness didn't seem to be a big bother. That, to Anita, was more than enough grounds to live a most rewarding life with the pastor. Happiness was what she had been looking for since Jerome died. Pastor McIntosh appeared to be the ideal candidate for that. The only remaining challenge for her was to rid herself of the menacing images of the past and Jerome.

Meanwhile, John had been summing up Anita's reaction to him on the journey. Being up front, he had all the time to think about Anita; constantly aware that she was only a few feet away from her was enough reason to think about her. John, like a stubborn mule, refused to accept that Anita had no interest whatsoever in him. What was the reason for that? He thought he had something to hang onto.

John was convinced that he was in Alfred's will. He firmly believed Anita would eventually have to befriend him in order to become a part of the inheritance. He was certain Alfred had done that deliberately. Had he known that Alfred had made up with his daughter, John would have second thoughts about a future with Anita. After many years of dedicated services to Alfred, John believed he had a legitimate claim to a portion of the estate.

John smiled once more, listening to Anita's calm voice behind him. *It is only a matter of time, Anita, before you come crawling to me, begging for my precious love.* John grinned with a silent grunt.

"I'm confident that you'll accomplish your task, son," Anita was saying.

"I'm glad you do, Mom, because I need whatever encouragement I can get."

"We're here to give you that. We'll give you as much as we can, remember Daddy's words."

John's ears picked up quickly the last sentence from Anita. What did she mean by Daddy's words? He must find out. Did Alfred change his mind about his grandson? Was he supporting him on this journey? He wished he knew the answer.

"I'll remember them. I must admit I do get a little nervous sometimes."

"That's expected, Andrew. You're going into a strange place but you'll get used to it," Pastor McIntosh tried to console him.

"Yuh wi do alright, sah," Jerry said.

"Glad to hear that from you, Jerry. It means a lot."

"If you're too busy to come to look us up, please let me know and we'll come," Anita suggested.

"That's reassuring. I know I may not be back until the New Year."

"We'll see how that goes."

Riding through the hills of the parish of Manchester wasn't that bad. The hilly region, nestled in thick vegetation, provided shade and coolness. At times, the buggy came to a crawl because of the rugged terrain. The worst thing that could have happened was for them to lose a wheel or horse. John skillfully guided the horses where he wanted them to go. He had been doing a splendid job, something most of them failed to notice.

Pastor McIntosh was the only person who seemed to recognize it. He was about to commend him at one time, but was distracted by something else, so he never got around to doing that.

Now would have been an ideal time to tell him because of the rough and winding roads they were encountering. Unfortunately, the pastor's thoughts weren't on the road. They had strayed to his dream last night. He allowed himself to think about it. The last word he woke up in time to hear coming from his mouth was Leonora. That word played with his mind.

She was something of a mystery. Leonora presented herself seemingly from out of nowhere. She was rather presumptuous for a first-time visitor. Firstly, she was full of praises for his sermon; secondly, she invited him for supper at the soonest possible date. On top of that, she suggested they get to know each other in a kind of flirtatious tone. No wonder she gave him a nightmare last night.

The pastor had to admit that she was an attractive woman. Suddenly, Anita entered his thoughts for the first time. Anita was also a beautiful woman. He looked across at her, the bumpy journey vibrating her whole body until it had put her to sleep. Her angelic and innocent look while sleeping brought an inward smile. Anita would be the perfect woman for any eligible bachelor. She had shrugged off the horrors of her past and was bent on starting a new life, he assumed. Anita had come to him looking for spiritual guidance and he had tried his best to impart it. Make no mistake about it, Anita had changed her whole outlook on life, he felt. She was more interested in the spiritual than the physical. Did she have another kind of interest—in him?

Admittedly, Pastor McIntosh never thought of that before. The emergence of Leonora had given him food—food for thought. From here on, he must be more conscious of any dialogue with the two women. He wouldn't want to jump the gun and make wrong assumptions. That could create a terrible mess; getting into it would be one thing, getting out would be another.

The sun was getting hotter. Anita woke up suddenly.

"Where are we?" Anita asked, stretching one of her hands in a yawn.

"I don't even know," the pastor replied.

"We should be going into Clarendon soon," John said from up front.

"Clarendon, St. Dorothy, St Catherine, St. Andrew and Kingston. It looks far away."

"Some of these parishes are small, remember?" Pastor McIntosh reminded her.

"Hmm, that's true. That makes it a little better."

"We're looking at three and a half more days."

"I can hardly wait to see Kingston," Andrew interjected.

"I'm getting a bit homesick," Anita said.

"Really. I'll miss conducting service on Sunday, but I don't mind the break at all."

"Lucky you. I'll miss service, too. I notice you had a new visitor on Sunday."

"Visitor? Oh! That young woman who came in?" Pastor McIntosh said, nodding.

"Who's she?" Anita asked anxiously. It was the best opportunity she would have to find out, she thought. It would be a relief to know.

"Leonora. Leonora Simmonds. She arrived from England last week with her father who'll be the new doctor for the area."

"Hmmm, that sounds interesting."

"A doctor is a most welcomed resident," the pastor said.

"I guess you could say the same for her, too," Anita mused, almost certain why she had made that statement.

"We'll see," Pastor McIntosh said with a smile.

CHAPTER 7

John Stewart and his crew of five had pushed very hard to be in Kingston as soon as possible. The outskirts of Kingston greeted their eyes at about midday on Friday. The vast stretch of land known as the Liguanea Plain was home for Kingston and neighboring St. Andrew. Further east was another small parish, Port Royal, the place that was home to notorious pirates such as Henry Morgan.

The city's landscape was very much different from the deep countryside. For one, there were more roads, houses, businesses, and people. The houses were far apart, but much smaller than the mansions of the plantations in the countryside.

The buggy slowed down its speed the moment John encountered other buggies and horses going in the same or opposite directions. The nearer they moved to the commercial area of Kingston, the busier it got. There were a lot of British citizens living in Kingston, and a considerable number of former slaves were around—walking, driving buggies, or riding horses.

"Keep going on this road, John. It will take you near to where we're going," Pastor McIntosh told him.

"Okay."

"This is your home for a while, Andrew. I hope you'll like it."

"I'll have to, Mom. It's not a matter of liking it, rather getting used to it."

Jerry and Simon were busy combing their area of vision for the usual and the unusual. It was their first big trip to the crowded city, and could be their only one. There were many people in Yardley Chase, who had never been to Kingston.

The journey to the Baptist Mission took them half an hour. The mission was a busy place. A hawk-nosed elderly looking man came out to greet them when the buggy pulled up on the premises.

"Oh! Goodness gracious! Wilfred, it's you," the man said, looking up at him before grabbing his hand.

"Bobby, oh my goodness! You're still around here?"

"By the grace of God I am, my dear boy. You look well," Robert Barnes said, holding on to his hand.

"You look well, too, Robert. I thought you had returned to Liverpool."

"Heh! Heh! Heh! I think I'll rot here in good ol' Kingston," he laughed.

Pastor McIntosh turned to introduce his traveling companions one by one. They were invited to come inside. They entered a large dining room with about a dozen people inside having a meal. Some of them were in pastoral attire.

An over exhausted traveling crew walked wearily into the room. They were drained of all their energy. Anita was the first to take a seat around one of the shining mahogany tables. Mahogany was a common tree in Jamaica, and its value as the prime wood for furniture had started to get attention because of its durability.

"It's nice here. Look at this table, it's beautiful," Anita said to Andrew as he sat down beside her.

"I like it already." Andrew smiled.

A stately looking man came toward them, followed by another. "Wilfred! It's really good to see you," he said, greeting him with a grip on the arm.

"Good to see you again," said the other.

"Lady and gentlemen, meet Pastor Isaac Thomas, the head of the Baptist Mission in Jamaica. I'm in his charge," Pastor McIntosh said.

They all shook hands, while the others who were nearby came over to be introduced. They talked for a few minutes until lunch came out. A hot meal of beef stew and potatoes was a treat for the travelers.

Anita and the rest were feeling more at home by late afternoon. Pastor McIntosh disappeared for a while and came to join them while they toured the premises. He caught up with Andrew and Anita, who had been trying to spend as much time as possible, together.

"Andrew, this will be your home for as long as you want to be here," the pastor told him through a wide grin.

"Is that invitation coming from the top?" Anita asked.

"As a matter of fact, yes. I just had a long talk with Pastor Thomas. I told him you'd be willing to pay a year, even two, in advance for room and board. He was a bit reluctant at first, but we agreed on that."

"I'm glad Grandpa decided to do that for me."

"Pastor Thomas wanted to know if you were interested in the ministry."

"What did you tell him?" Anita asked curiously.

"I explained that you don't want to do that directly at the present time. However, your sole interest is the welfare of former slaves, and you believe the church is a good foundation to start from."

"I don't know how to thank you, Pastor. You couldn't have said it better."

"I agree," Anita said.

"I can assure you that the church is with you on this. In fact, some of its pastors have been active in this area already, both in the east and west."

"Hmmm, that's encouraging to hear."

"Andrew, I'm glad everything is moving ahead as we planned. I don't know how to thank Pastor for all of what he's doing."

"His blessings will come from above."

"You're already sounding like a preacher," Pastor McIntosh said.

"Well, I'll have to start somewhere. When you all plan to leave?"

"You want to get rid of us already?" Anita asked.

"C'mon, Mom. I'm missing you already," he said, putting his arm around her shoulders. "I don't mean it that way for one moment."

"I was only kidding, Andrew."

"The others are enjoying themselves. I'm going to see what they are up to," Andrew said, leaving them standing together.

"There goes one young man with a bright future."

"I'm proud of him. I wish his father could see him now."

"You have every reason to be proud of your son."

"Are there any women living here?" Anita asked, trying to change the subject.

"Of course, the women in the office work and live here. Come, let me introduce you to them."

Pastor and Anita walked over to the administrative office, where a petite, reddish haired woman in her late thirties greeted them. She was rather friendly and introduced herself even before Pastor McIntosh could open his mouth.

"I'm Elizabeth Cameron. It's a pleasure," she said, extending her hand. Elizabeth's blue eyes examined her thoroughly before she turned her attention to Wilfred.

"Nice meeting you," Anita said.

"It's good to see you again, Pastor," Elizabeth said.

"It's nice to see you, too. Where are the others?" the pastor asked, looking around the office.

"I'm the only one here today. Erica is down with the flu. Madge has a day off."

"How's Kingston these days?"

"The usual, except for the politics. Is this your first visit here...?"

"Sorry, it's Anita..."

"Are you staying by me tonight?"

"Er...I don't know."

"Now that you've made the offer, I would imagine that's where she'll be."

"Our women visitors usually stay with us, right?" Elizabeth asked, as if she was seeking the pastor's approval.

"As far as I can remember, yes."

"The office will soon close, Anita. You can wait if you want, and we'll go over together."

"That sounds fine to me."

"Me, too," Pastor McIntosh said.

Peter Bradley had been riding all morning. He couldn't face another boring and agonizing weekend alone again. He wanted to see Anita badly. The young barrister left Black River early morning, in order to cover as much ground as possible before the sun reached the midway mark in the sky. Peter had been riding nonstop all morning. When he took a break at midday, it was evident that he would have to move very fast to be in Yardley Chase before nightfall. He was confident his horse would fulfill his wish.

Peter's confidence paid off. The mountainous terrain that descended into Lover's Leap had started to appear dark when he approached Yardley Chase. The sun was nowhere to be seen. The sound of whistling crickets and croaking frogs had already started to transform the tranquil atmosphere into an enchanting melody.

Peter rode through the gate at Jack's Place with the pace of a rider being chased by bandits. He tightened the reins a few yards before he reached the stable. Had anyone seen him coming, they would have wondered why the rush.

Lynda heard the galloping hooves, and parted the curtain of the kitchen window to identify the rider. Anita couldn't have been back already, unless of course something had happened. She became nervous when she saw no one. Lynda waited a few minutes. There was no knock on the door, prompting her to look outside. As she grabbed the doorknob to open it, the familiar figure of Peter loomed in front of her.

"Hey...what...I didn't expect you...is...is something wrong?" she queried, opening the door wider to let him in. Alfred was coming down the stairs at the same time.

"No! No, no...I was bored; I thought I would ride up here for the weekend." He grinned, wiping sweat from his forehead.

"You need no invitation, Peter," Alfred said, coming up to them.

"That was nice of you, Peter. Come on in, you must be starving," Lynda said.

"The house is too quiet. Where's everybody?"

"Oh! Anita, Andrew, and John are in Kingston. Andrew decided to leave, and they all accompanied him," Alfred said.

Peter raised his eyebrows, disappointment clearly written in his face. The sole reason for coming there was Anita and he was hearing that she was nearly one hundred miles away in Kingston.

"Good for him. I'm happy for that bright young man. He has a goal. I think this is the time to pursue it."

"I know you were expecting to see Anita," Lynda said, offering him a chair around the dining table.

"Well, I couldn't deny that. I was looking forward to seeing her."

"She should be back around the middle of next week."

"You two are getting close?" Alfred asked.

Peter paused before putting a piece of yam in his mouth. "I'm trying. She needs a little more time. I respect that."

"She told you that?" Lynda asked.

"Yes. I've no problem there."

"She has changed a lot, Peter. I believe she has matured. What may be utmost on her mind is the need to settle down," Alfred said.

"Give her another year, she'll be all yours," Lynda said, bringing him a cup of tea. She made one for Alfred, too.

"I hope I'm that lucky," Peter blurted out.

"What do you mean?" Lynda asked.

"Oh! Nothing! All I'm saying is that I'll be a lucky man."

"You certainly will be. I cannot imagine why a slave would have such an impact on her?" Lynda said. "I mean he's not alive."

"She saw him jump," Alfred said.

"And with another slave," Peter said.

"Jealousy was killing her. His death made matters worse," Alfred said.

"The Kingston trip will be good for her. The exposure is good," Lynda said.

"Let us hope she doesn't fall in love," Peter grinned, jealousy in his voice.

"Hmmm, don't worry about that. Pastor McIntosh is there to straighten her out, should she fall into such a situation."

"Pastor McIntosh! He went with her, too?" Peter asked wide-eyed.

"Yes," Lynda answered softly.

Elizabeth was turning out to be a very interesting woman. Over the supper table, she poured out all her life story to Anita, including that of a broken relationship with a young pastor who had moved to the north coast. Her story aroused Anita's interest. The other two women had retired to bed, leaving them alone in the kitchen.

Not surprisingly, Elizabeth had a kind of dossier on Pastor McIntosh. She knew where he was born, schooled, worked and his last relationship with a woman.

"What happened?" Anita asked, too anxious to hear more.

"Cathy wanted to stay in England. Wilfred was adamant he would spend the rest of his life in the tropics."

"There was no room for compromise?"

"Not from Cathy. I remember her from school days. She and Wilfred were always together. If you saw one you could expect to see the other. After school, the relationship blossomed into a full-blown romance. There were even plans to marry..."

"And..."

"Wilfred went to study theology. It changed everything."

"How?"

"It was as if he was transformed. After a while, all that mattered to him was the church. An opportunity came up for him to come to Jamaica; he snatched it right away. I came a month after him. I left England without even knowing he was here. Before I left I bumped into Cathy one day in London. She told me everything. She had heard from Wilfred only once."

Anita didn't know what to think. "Do they correspond?"

"That I don't know but I have doubts about that," Elizabeth said, sounding as if she was abreast of the whole affair.

"What about here? Is he seeing anyone?"

"Ha! You're interested, aren't you?"

The question caught Anita off guard. "I'll admit I like him. Let's leave it at that," she said, wondering if she should have said all of that.

"If he's not seeing anyone in Yardley Chase, I hardly think his mind is on women right now. Of course, he could be corresponding with someone here in Kingston. There are quite a few single ladies around; however, the distance would be an inhibiting factor in such a relationship. Would you like some tea?"

"Thanks."

Elizabeth continued the conversation while making the tea. She, too, was enjoying the talk. "Pastor is a nice man. I would love to see him start a family. I guess his dedication to the church must be his main priority at this time."

"He works hard. I can see that. The people in Yardley Chase do appreciate his work."

"He worked here for a while. He worked so hard they never wanted him to leave. However, Wilfred insisted that he wanted to serve out in the countryside."

"I know he enjoys what he's doing and that's good."

Elizabeth stopped what she had been doing. She stared at Anita. "Tell me, Anita, honestly, do you fancy him, or...er, would you want him for a husband?"

Anita looked away from her gaze. If she was surprised by the question, her face was hiding that picture. In the short time she had known Elizabeth, she summed her up as a woman who was very straightforward. She made good conversation. As an added bonus, she could learn a lot from her. As a result, Anita was going to lay it out all on her.

"There's another man who has asked for my friendship," she said, rising from her seat.

"And..."

"I told him I needed more time."

"Because of Wilfred?"

"I don't know myself. Sometimes I tend to feel that way. There are other times I'm utterly confused."

"How long do you think he'll wait?"

"He'll wait. There aren't many women in the countryside to choose from."

"Is he handsome?" Elizabeth asked, smiling.

"He's an attractive man...a barrister."

"Hmmm. If you don't need him, please let me know," she said, looking from one corner of her eye while waiting for her reaction.

"Are you looking?"

"I'm getting old y'know. There aren't many to choose from. I may have to start getting serious."

"Are you looking a pastor?"

"I think so."

"Peter isn't religious."

"That's his name, Peter?"

"Yes. I know someone else who's looking."

"Who?" she asked quickly.

Anita laughed almost aloud. This was a way of making up to John. "He's a nice man who has always been crazy about me but that's a very long, long story."

"What's his name?"

"John Stewart, and guess what?"

"Yes."

"He's right here. He took us to Kingston. John has been my father's overseer for as long as I can remember. He may be a few years older than you, very loyal and is longing for a wife."

"Church?" Elizabeth sat down beside her.

"He's not interested in church, although you could get him interested."

"Well, Anita, can you introduce me tomorrow? When are you leaving?"

"On Monday."

"I'll have two days to get to know him better."

"Good." Anita was delighted. There was no doubt that John had been dropping some hints that told her he was again trying with her.

"Let's sleep on that. Forget Peter, you can keep him," she teased.

Meanwhile, many miles away in Yardley Chase, Peter was having a restless night. He was tormented. Sleep wasn't coming his way. Tried as he might, Peter couldn't stop thinking of the few days he had spent with Anita on his previous visit. He could hear her voice, laughter, and the smooth talk. That was a woman! What else could he possibly want in life more than to be married to this woman? He was willing to wait, even if it meant another few years.

Peter decided to go for a ride early Saturday morning. He told Lynda and Alfred, while eating breakfast, that he would take a ride to Top Hill this time. He had always been travelling west; this time he would go east. They welcomed his little adventure because they hated to see him bored to death around the house. The absence of Anita had an impact on him, unlike previous visits when he came strictly on business, working throughout the weekend.

Peter galloped away to the east with his horse eager to go wherever he was commanded. Along the way, he saw several people carrying produce on their heads. He assumed they were on their way to some kind of market. In some instances, donkeys and mules trotted away laden with all kinds of foodstuff.

The scene made his trip even more interesting. For one thing, the farmers and vendors were happy, greeting one another whenever they met. Peter found that interesting, forcing him to stop his horse to listen to the exchange of greetings. While he was sitting unmoved in his saddle, he noticed someone else was doing the same thing. It was a woman. At first, Peter thought she was looking in his direction.

Leonora Simmonds' inquisitive and curious eyes were drawn to the figure sitting on the horse in the middle of the road, a few yards away from the market. She had gone there to buy some vegetables, and was about to guide her horse in the opposite direction. However, she couldn't help noticing among the crowd, a stationary horse with a rider in the saddle. She could see he was British, at least he was dressed like one. She had every intention to find out whether he spoke like one.

"Good morning," Leonora said as she approached him.

"Oh! Good morning, m'lady. How are you?"

"I'm doing fine and you?"

"I'm fine. Peter Bradley is the name," he said, extending his hand.

He is indeed British, she thought. "Leonora Simmonds. Do you live around here?"

"No, ma'am. I live in Black River," he said, pointing in that direction. I'm visiting for the weekend. You're from here, I suppose," Peter said, smiling with confidence that his assumption was correct.

"I am. My father and I came in from England last week."

"Oh! You're new," he exclaimed.

"You could say that."

"I'm not really new. I'm the barrister for Jack's Place, a nearby plantation. I come here from time to time on business."

"That's interesting. I'm getting to know Yardley Chase each day. It's a nice area of the island."

"I agree. It's rather cool. It's not hot like other areas. I like the greenery, the lush vegetation, especially the fruit trees. I was going for a ride in this direction because each time I come here I always stop at Yardley Chase."

"I'll soon have to start exploring myself."

"Have you started a job as yet?"

"No. I haven't been looking either. I want to settle down a bit before I start doing that."

Peter was summing her up while they talked. *A rather interesting woman*, he thought, *friendly, maybe lonely.* "What will you do?"

"I can teach."

"Have you ever worked in an office?"

"No, I could learn easily. Why?"

"I was thinking that you could pick up a job easy in Black River, at one of those barrister or shipping company offices."

"There are jobs in Black River?" Leonora asked. "How far away is Black River?"

"About twenty miles. It's a busy little town. Would you move down there?"

"Hmmm. I wasn't thinking about that. My father is a doctor who has his work cut out here for him. I don't believe he would want to leave anytime soon."

The horses began to trot away from where they had stopped. They continued their conversation while the horses moved slowly.

"He's a doctor. That makes it even better. Black River could do well with another doctor."

"Oh! C'mon, Peter, don't start giving me ideas," she said, calling his name in a tone that suggested that she had known him for a long time.

"I'm sorry, I shouldn't be doing that. Forget it, I was only kidding."

"It sounds feasible, though. The only shortcoming is that these people need medical services, too. There isn't a doctor within twenty miles of here."

"You're right," Peter admitted.

"When are you leaving for Black River?"

"I was thinking of tomorrow or Monday morning."

"Well, if you are here tomorrow why not come over for tea," she asked.

"Hmmm, where do you live?"

"Over there," Leonora said, pointing to a house in the distance.

"You're nearby."

"That's right. How far is Jack's Place?"

"Less than a mile. It's near Lover's Leap."

"I have heard that name. I hear it's an interesting place, something about slaves jumping to death from there."

"That happened some time ago for real. Anita, the daughter of the owner of Jack's Place, was there when it happened."

"Do you know Anita?" Leonora asked hastily.

"Of course. I'm certain you'll meet her soon. She's a rather interesting woman...like you."

Leonora blushed. "Oh! Thank you for that compliment. You appear to be a nice person, too."

"Huh, that's rather nice of you."

"My father would be delighted to meet you. A doctor and a barrister would make a good team. Lots to talk about huh?"

"We will see." Peter grinned.

Peter accompanied her to the gate of the house, and resumed his journey. Leonora watched him go with admiration. *Where did that one emerge from?* she wondered.

Peter rode two more miles, the thought of the woman he had met a few minutes ago nibbling at his mind. She was as interesting as she looked. Leonora was new. That was what made him somewhat interested to learn more about her. Without any hesitation, he would leave on Monday, rather than Sunday. There was no way he could turn down that invitation to tea.

Peter left Jack's Place for Leonora's house on Sunday afternoon. It wouldn't have been a wise idea to inform Lynda or Alfred of his mission; he told them he was going for a ride. Lynda sympathized with his boredom, offering to ride with him. However, Peter emphasized that he was okay.

Dr. Simmonds was a very jovial man. He met Peter with outstretched arms. They hit it off right away. Their conversation went from British politics to Jamaican politics, from slavery to emancipation. They must have been talking for about an hour before Leonora interrupted.

"Dad, Peter says there are jobs in Black River." She had run home excited yesterday to tell her father about this Englishman she had met. But she never discussed his job proposal with him. Leonora wanted to hear his reaction.

"Jobs? That's good to hear. I'm quite comfortable here, though. Furthermore, there's no doctor in this area."

"Women can get jobs there, too," she said, eyeing Peter for his reaction.

"Don't worry, you'll get a job around here," Dr. Simmonds assured her.

"And if I don't..."

"Well, we'll see what happens," Dr. Simmonds said, flashing his hand as if he wanted to discontinue discussing jobs.

The doctor and Peter resumed their conversation. This time, it went on for another two hours. Leonora was bored, and it was a relief when Peter indicated it was time to go. At least she had the opportunity of accompanying him to the gate.

"That was some talk?" Leonora told him when they reached the gate.

"Well, your father is a rather interesting man. I can see he's very knowledgeable about the tropics. He likes to talk, there's nothing wrong with that." Peter grinned.

"Did you enjoy the evening after all?" Leonora's eyes surveyed his face; Peter was conscious of her curiosity. It made him feel awkward. Peter tried to walk beside her to avoid her stare. He kept walking even when she tried to stop to talk.

"I must admit the visit was a breather."

"What do you mean?" she said, stopping in her tracks again. The gate was only a few yards away.

"I was getting a bit bored back there."

"No female company over there?"

Peter never expected that kind of question. Did she know Anita? "I don't know if that would make a difference," he remarked, speaking tactfully in order not to give away too much information.

"Young females, I should say. Wouldn't that make a difference?"

"Hmmm. I guess it depends on the individual." Again, Peter tried to be very reserved in his answer. This woman was poking for information. He had no idea why.

"It would be hard for me to imagine that you came all the way from Black River to be bored?"

As evasive as Peter as tried to be, Leonora wasn't giving up. "A change of atmosphere could be well worth the trip."

"That may be so, but tell me, are there a lot of young women in Yardley Chase?" Leonora was up to some mischief here. On second thoughts, he should turn the tides and tell her what she probably wanted to hear.

"You know there are quite a few around...very beautiful, too."

"Hmmm. You haven't found any as yet?" she asked, waiting for his reaction.

"Who says I'm looking?"

"C'mon, Peter, do you take me seriously? I was only kidding."

Kidding to get information, Peter said to himself. "That's a smart way to look at it."

"When will you come again?"

"I don't know."

"I guess if you have some interest here you could be required to come anytime," Leonora said with a forced smile.

"Alfred runs a huge plantation. He constantly needs legal matters to be dealt with. I come instead to save him the trouble coming all the way to Black River. And to be honest with you, I don't mind it at all."

"You seem to be dedicated to your work."

"I am," he emphasized. "It's my life."

"Whenever you come, please feel free to call on me. Will you?" she asked sincerely.

"I will for sure. I can see you need to make some friends. Furthermore, you do know how to make good conversation…like your father."

"Like father, like daughter," Leonora laughed. "I wish you had more time in Yardley Chase. The next time you should stay a little longer."

"You know I may have to do that. Now that you are around, there's reason to spend some more time, if that's okay with you."

"Okay? I would say that's the best piece of news I've received since being here. Imagine a young, handsome barrister from all the way in Black River going to call on me. Isn't that something to talk about? Hmm, it's a pity I don't have anyone, except Dad, to relay this news to. I hope I don't have sleepless nights over this and get so anxious that you'll seem to take a long time to come," Leonora said in a theatrical way.

"You should go into acting. Have you ever done any work in the theater?" Peter asked, not knowing how to respond to her statement.

"I sure did in school."

"You should take it up here."

"I would have to go to Kingston. I think I prefer it around here."

"It's nice here. I wouldn't give it away for anything."

"You're right, Peter. I've never been to Black River; however, I have a funny feeling I would go there. I like the sea."

"If you walk through the back door of my office you step right onto the shore," Peter said, leaning against the huge gate.

"Is that an invitation?" Leonora asked.

"Well, I think it would be good for you to visit to see what it's like. There's no harm in that."

"I would've to talk with Dad."

"He, too, would want to pay a visit."

"That's an idea. Are there nice inns there?"

"My dear, my house has four bedrooms."

"Peter, Dad is going to be elated to hear this."

The weekend went by as quickly as it had come. Anita found it hard to believe that it was over. She was on her way back to Yardley Chase, leaving behind the only physical evidence of Jerome—Andrew. It was on occasions like this that her relationship with Jerome brought back cherished memories. Her only reason for comfort was that Andrew had started to pursue his dream.

Since they left Kingston, all they had been doing was traveling, sleeping, eating, and on a few occasions, talking. Pastor McIntosh did most of the talking. Anita always got involved. John made a few comments, but for the most part, Simon and Jerry remained silent as usual.

The trip to Kingston was fruitful in many ways. Besides transporting Andrew, Anita had learned a lot about the pastor from Elizabeth. That was very important to her. Anita was satisfied that Andrew would be taken care of at the mission. He was in capable hands. There was little doubt about that. And last, but not least, before she boarded the buggy in Kingston, Elizabeth came up to thank her for introducing John. Somewhat baffled at first, Anita read between the lines and concluded that somehow a spark had been ignited between the two. Anita thought she got confirmation yesterday when she glanced across at a smiling John. The funny thing was that he was smiling to himself, for a while, too. Even after that, she noticed a change in his attitude; he was more jovial, kept saying his trip to Kingston would always be a memorable one. Was John still dreaming, or had someone indeed walked into his life?

The traveling party approached the descent of Spur Tree Hills. The view of almost the entire parish of St. Elizabeth was breathtaking. The Santa Cruz mountain range was there for all to see, as it stretched some thirty miles from north to south before it started disappearing into a concealed Lover's Leap. It was one huge green mass below, except for the dark patches made by shadows from the mid-afternoon sun. It was humid as the weary travelers were trying to reach home before dusk. The travel from Kingston had started to take its toll from yesterday. Jerry and Simon were fast asleep, despite the blaring sun. John, everyone would care to admit, had been doing a fantastic job of controlling the buggy.

"I can see you're longing for home," Pastor McIntosh said to Anita.

"I wish I was home," she said.

"You'll be soon," he assured her.

"This view is amazing. I can almost see Yardley Chase from here," she said, pointing in that direction.

"It's truly beautiful. Are you missing Andrew?"

"I am missing him, there's no denying that. The days ahead are going to be very difficult for me."

"If you want, I can come over whenever you wish."

Anita wanted to hear more statements like that. In fact, she felt they were long overdue. Earlier on the journey, she had started to wonder what she could do to entice the pastor to visit her more often. With that statement, she needed to look no further.

"That's very kind of you. Anytime you wish you could come. I'll need the help." She smiled.

"I know how it feels to miss someone."

"You do?" Anita asked, remembering what Elizabeth had told her about Wilfred leaving London for Jamaica.

"Some years ago, I had to make a decision similar to yours. It brought pain only for a while. I got very busy in my work, and the pain soon disappeared.

Anita realized he was talking about the same incident Elizabeth had told her. "Was it someone close to you?" she asked.

"Yes, you could say that. In the end, God was the winner."

"I see. I admire you for that..."

"For what?"

"The zeal, the drive you have for putting God above all things."

"Don't you think he deserves that kind of treatment? After all, he's the Creator."

"Of course I do. You cannot imagine the change that has been taking place in my life ever since I started coming to church," Anita said, staring at him.

"You don't have to tell me...I know, I know. I can see it, Anita. I know God is working in your life. My plea to you is to continue to grow to worship him in spirit and in truth."

"Even my parents have noticed the change."

"And that's good, too. What about them, though? Time is moving on. I'm concerned that they don't seem to be doing anything about their spiritual lives."

"Mom is willing. I don't know about Dad. It will take a little time."

"Yes I know. Let's hope it won't be too late."

CHAPTER 8

Lynda was getting used to the unusual quietness around the house since two of its regular occupants weren't around. This afternoon was unusually quiet, though. Alfred said he wasn't feeling well and went upstairs to lie down for a while. Downstairs, Lynda tried to find something to do in order to occupy her time. If her reckoning was right, Anita should be back this afternoon. She could hardly wait to hear more about Andrew's trip.

Lynda sat in the kitchen for a while. The maids had already left. She didn't mind being by herself to meditate for a while over the events of the past three weeks. The first thing that hit her inviting mind was Peter's visit over the weekend. It was a disappointment for her. If she was that disappointed, Lynda could well imagine how Peter had felt with Anita's absence. There was little Lynda could do; she was helpless. That predicament made her as worthless as she could ever imagine. She was about to turn her thoughts to Pastor McIntosh's kind gesture to take them into Kingston, when the creaking sound of a buggy's wheels caught her attention. Lynda, anxious as ever, dashed to the window, her feet stomping on the wooden floor. Her eyes caught the arriving party; she liked what she saw. Anita was back!

Somehow, Anita's return without Andrew brought a certain solemnity to the dying afternoon. Lynda sensed that the moment she saw John, Anita and the boys approaching the house. Pastor McIntosh didn't return to Jack's Place with them.

"Thank God you're all back safe and sound," a relieved Lynda said.

"We're glad to be back, Mom." Anita walked up to her mother and they hugged each other.

"Thanks, John…Jerry…Simon, you all did a splendid job. Did everything go as planned?"

"Yes, Mom. Everything went as planned. Pastor McIntosh took care of everything. I've all the confidence that Andrew is in good hands. We have to be grateful to him for that. Where's Dad?"

"Oh! He's lying down—a bit tired."

"Is he all right?"

"Yes. He's all right. John, you all want to come in for some tea?"

"Thanks, Lynda, that will be good."

The kitchen became a beehive of activity, with the knocking of pots, pans and cups and saucers. Suddenly, the noise was drowned out by a scream from upstairs. Anita came rushing down the stairs hysterically.

Everyone turned their attention to Anita, who by that time was making some inaudible sounds as she tried to make sense.

"Mom…Dad…Dad…" she said, pointing upstairs.

"What about him?" Lynda asked nervously.

"Come…he…" Anita's voice trembled. "Come…" She grabbed her hand and started to lead Lynda upstairs. John, fearing the look on her face, darted ahead of them. The stairs appeared flat by the way in which John conquered its elevating slant.

They all entered the room to see John trying to wake Alfred. There was no movement from him. It took a few minutes for John to face the reality that what he was trying to revive was no longer a living person. Alfred was dead.

John turned around. They all saw the look in his eyes. Lynda covered her face with her hands. Anita made a step backward and screamed like she never did before. Simon and Jerry looked at each other. They, too, wanted to cry. The screams and crying got so loud that even the maids heard them from their quarters. They came to be greeted with the bad news—the most powerful and richest man in Yardley Chase was dead. The man, whose plantation was the lifeblood of the small community, was no more. A plantation owner, surviving all the rigors of slavery right through to emancipation, had passed on.

The news of Alfred's demise spread throughout Yardley Chase like wildfire. Pastor McIntosh, a tired as he was, came quickly. He found a family stricken with grief, trying to come to grips with sudden death. He tried to comfort them with words that Alfred had gone on to a better place. Lynda and Anita were devastated.

Pastor McIntosh sent Jerry and Simon to inform the new physician Dr. Simmonds of Alfred's death. The doctor, accompanied by his daughter Leonora, arrived at Jack's Place within an hour. Lynda told him what happened.

"He died peacefully. I'm sorry," Dr. Simmonds told Lynda, Anita and Pastor McIntosh. "He might have had a massive stroke while he was asleep. He felt no pain."

Leonora stood beside her father while he was talking to them. The puzzle of the mystery woman had been solved. Through the introductions, Anita had learned the woman's name, and that she was the doctor's daughter. But that was of little concern to Anita, at least for now. Her father was dead. What could be more important?

The house was almost full with people in a matter of hours. Pastor McIntosh used the opportunity to introduce the doctor and his daughter to the community. Anita bumped into them several times, but the death of her father dealt such a blow that Leonora's presence with the pastor meant nothing to her at that moment.

Alfred was buried the following afternoon. Yardley Chase had its biggest funeral. Plantation owners, former slaves, laborers, friends, and associates from near and far came for the funeral on a gray and dull afternoon. The sky opened up and the rains came with a thud as soon as Pastor McIntosh finished the funeral service. The huge crowd had to seek shelter at Jack's Place, inside the house, barn, and storeroom and wherever people could stay without getting wet.

Yardley Chase had lost a stalwart, a pioneer of plantation life. As bad as conditions were in this post-slavery period, Alfred had a good reputation for being kind-hearted and fair. He was one of the few owners in the southern section of the island who was known to hire more laborers than he actually needed after emancipation. All his good qualities came out in the eulogy delivered by his able and long-time overseer, John Stewart. There was no better person to do such an honor. Since John came from England, the only job he ever had was with Alfred. John broke down and wept bitterly after the eulogy.

The ensuing week in Yardley Chase was one of conversation and reflection on the life of Alfred. There was a large gathering one night when Lynda invited the entire community over to Jack's Place. Many stories were recalled on life's experiences with Alfred. They were all positive. They gave Anita and Lynda comfort that Alfred had such an impact on the community.

Alfred's family was small. Andrew's absence added to the sense of loss. Pastor McIntosh was very supportive, while John's involvement in the funeral arrangements was beyond compensation, monetarily or otherwise.

Peter Mackay rode into Jack's Place the following Wednesday afternoon. He had received word of Alfred's death. Peter waited a few days before coming. He thought it best to do that because he was executor of his will. It was definitely a business trip. As much as Peter wanted to see Anita, he would try to keep it that way.

Leonora came to mind while he was on his way to Jack's Place. However, the moment he saw Anita standing in the doorway at the front of the house, it wasn't difficult to get Leonora out of his thoughts. They greeted each other with a hug.

"I'm sorry," Peter said. "He was a good man."

"He was...he was a good father, too."

"How are you making out?"

"It was difficult to believe at first. I came back from Kingston to find him sleeping...and he...was dead," Anita said, bursting into tears.

Peter held her again. Lynda joined them as they released each other from the embrace.

"Hi, Peter. Thanks for coming."

"I'm sorry, Lynda."

"In the midst of life there's death. It's a reality we can never get used to, no matter how often it occurs. Alfred has gone on before us. It's a pity we didn't get to say goodbye."

"He died in his sleep?"

"Yes. Anita found him. Come inside."

They talked way into the night then retired to bed exhausted as ever. Peter found himself awake in the middle of the night troubled by his next task—the reading of Alfred's last will and testimony. A confused Peter concluded that he should have waited another week. Perhaps he should hang around for a few days before making any move. Peter was able to do that without any problem whatsoever, except for Saturday morning, when John met him at the stable. Peter was getting a horse ready to take Anita for the usual morning ride when John walked up to greet him. He posed the question right away.

"When is the will being read?" he asked, as serious as a judge.

"Soon. Why?"

"Curious, I guess."

"Hmmm. The family needs some time to recover from the shock of his death," Peter said, wondering about John's lack of compassion for a grieving family.

"You're right. I'm sorry for being insensitive to that."

"Have a good day." Peter walked away, leaving John standing there.

John was convinced that something was in that will for him. It had to be; his many years of loyalty to Alfred justified that. He had a reason to be anxious.

Peter hadn't been to church in a long time. He knew he had to break that dry spell, on Sunday morning. Anita and Lynda were going to church, therefore, it was only logical that he accompanied them. Peter was glad he did; the service provided hope through Jesus Christ, both for the living and for the dead.

Anita was standing with Peter while Lynda was talking with Pastor McIntosh. Leonora, who Anita didn't see at the service, came up to them.

"Hi, Anita. Hi, Peter. I didn't know you were here," she said with a wide smile on her face.

Anita was shocked to learn they knew each other.

"Oh! Yes I'm here."

"You two know each other?" Anita asked.

"We met the other day," Leonora said. "Dad enjoyed his company very much," she teased.

"Oh," Anita said.

"Are you all ready?" Lynda called out to them.

"Yes, Mom."

"Do come by to visit before you leave, Peter. Dad wants to discuss that Black River trip with you. Take care of him, Anita. I'm sorry about your father."

Anita managed a smile before joining her mother. Leonora had the full attention of Pastor McIntosh in no time.

"What was that all about?" Anita asked Peter.

"Hmmm. An unpredictable woman I might say."

"How did you meet?"

"While you were in Kingston I came to look for you. Did you know that?"

"No," a startled Anita said.

"Alfred's death was much more important. I understand perfectly. I came on the weekend only to learn you were gone to Kingston with Andrew."

"I'm sorry about that," Anita said, her eyes searching the room for Leonora. She was engaged in what looked like an interesting dialogue with the pastor. He was listening attentively to whatever poison or nourishment that was coming from her lips, Anita thought, wondering why she didn't like her.

"That's okay. You had to go. Anyway, one day I went for a ride only to meet this young woman, quite friendly, ready to talk. I learned her father was a doctor who arrived a few weeks ago. She invited me to tea. That was it!" Peter explained, almost throwing up his hands in the air.

"What's this going to Black River bit?"

"Oh! I told her a little about Black River. As she's looking for a job she thought she may find something there."

"Uh-huh, so she wants to come to spend some time down there."

"I guess. She means nothing to me, Anita, you know I care about you."

Anita didn't answer. She joined her mother heading for the door. A hand held onto hers a few feet away from the door. Anita turned to see Pastor McIntosh smiling at him.

"I didn't get in a word but how was the day?" Peter had disappeared through the door.

"Great, Pastor! That was a good sermon. It gives hope to all of us."

"To God be the glory."

"When are you coming by?"

"Ah! I didn't want to impose too much because I know grieving families need some space sometimes."

"C'mon, you're always welcome, you know that. Your presence means a lot to us, especially at this time."

"Can I come this afternoon? I see you have company. Please let me know if I'm imposing too much?"

"That's fine, Pastor. Dinner is waiting." She smiled.

"I like your spirit, Anita. I can see you're trying to move on."

"Thanks. Life is too short to waste it. You know I've wasted a lot already," Anita said, avoiding his eyes.

"I think you're doing remarkably well. You'll even do better now that your ability to be an independent woman will work well for you," Pastor advised her, sounding like a father talking to a teenage daughter.

"Years are catching up on me, too. I believe I'll have to start deciding what I'm going to do about my life."

"I'm quite positive that you'll soon find a young man whom you'll marry to start a family."

Anita never expected that statement from Pastor McIntosh. However, she assumed he was using the opportunity to tell her that was something she should be thinking about, with Alfred not around anymore. In other words, Anita needed someone to take care of her.

"Hmmm, it's not that easy y'know."

"You mean finding someone?"

"Exactly."

"Peter seems to be a nice young man."

"Peter! He sure is..." Anita said, looking around as if he was nearby. "He's a good man that would make a good husband." She waited for his reaction but there was none, except for a warm smile on his charming face.

"What's the problem, my dear?"

"I believe I have someone else in mind." She blushed.

"You're kidding me, aren't you?"

"No, I'm not," Anita said jokingly.

"Well, well, who might that be? Is it someone I know?" Pastor McIntosh was intrigued by their dialogue. As far as he could remember, it was the first time the two of them were discussing such a sensitive subject. And of all the places to be discussing it—church, right after service. *Grief could be playing a part in this sudden turn of reasoning,* he thought.

"There's no way for you not to know him. I'll leave it at that...don't go around guessing because you might be in for a surprise. I'm certain you'll select the wrong person."

"That sounds like homework, or something to bear in mind in the event that I might have to conduct a wedding service," he teased.

"You'll have to be there, unless of course you want to miss the time of your life," she laughed. "As a matter of fact, you're going to be there," she added facetiously.

"Something like that could never miss me. Who'll join your hand...who'll conduct such a ceremony anyway? Unless you have someone else in mind."

"You know what, that may very well happen," she laughed heartily. "I'll definitely see to it."

"Your Mom must be waiting."

I'm waiting for you, Anita said to herself. *Jerome, please understand,* she added. "See you at dinner."

"Later, Anita," Pastor McIntosh said, watching her go.

Anita stepped outside to be greeted by Leonora talking to Peter. Lynda was nearby talking with some other people. A streak of jealousy ran through Anita's body as quickly as a flash of lightning. *Is it truly jealousy?* Anita wondered. Why should she be anyway, when only moments ago she wanted so much to continue that conversation with Pastor?

The pain of her father's death was lingering on. The years of animosity between them could have driven a wedge of guilt to any future relationship she had with a man. They had made up shortly before her departure to Kingston. On her return, Anita was looking forward to a very fruitful daughter-father relationship, making up for the lost years. Again, like Jerome, death brought a sudden blow to her dreams. The hurt was intense, and the guilt had begun to take its toll on her. Anita was searching unconsciously for a way to soothe the pain. Anita needed as many male friends as possible, at this time, whether they were interested in her or not. No doubt, Leonora made her feel jealous.

"Are you ready?" Peter asked Anita, speaking over Leonora's shoulder as she came near them.

"I'm starving."

"It's good you're eating," Leonora said.

"If I weren't I would be in the ground, too," Anita said, not looking at her. The first day she saw Leonora, Anita started to compare herself. Leonora was younger, very pretty, a little too friendly. She could make friends as well as enemies easily. That troubled Anita.

"Cheer up, life goes on. We should get to know each other; after all, there aren't many young women like us around," Leonora suggested.

"We'll be seeing you. Say hello to your father for me," Peter said, holding Anita by the hand.

"When will you be coming over?" she asked after him.

"I don't know."

Pastor McIntosh came up beside Leonora. Anita looked back

at her; her heart raced faster the moment she saw Pastor McIntosh joining Leonora. Anita wished she could find an excuse to go back. Lynda was walking ahead of her with some people. By now, most of the people had drifted away. As they turned the corner to lose sight of the church, Anita dropped her handbag on the ground behind her, deliberately, in order to get one last look. Peter retrieved the bag quickly but not before Anita glanced at the church to see Leonora and Pastor McIntosh talking. Jealousy burned the walls of her stomach. She felt sick.

CHAPTER 9

The Sunday afternoon dragged on lazily into dinnertime. Anita waited impatiently to see whether Pastor McIntosh would indeed keep his promise. He was a man of his word; Anita had no reason to doubt him; however, jealousy had been controlling her emotions. Leonora could easily have encouraged him to come for dinner instead.

Anita used every opportunity to maintain dialogue with Peter. She did that for good reason because she couldn't guarantee that kind of conversation when Wilfred arrived. John joined them, too. They did have a lively discussion, mainly about the trip to Kingston, until it was time to eat. Pastor McIntosh came a few minutes before they were ready.

Dinner was a sumptuous meal of beef and potatoes, yams, corn, and carrots. A bottle of wine that was placed on the table disappeared in no time. Anita and Lynda were having their first full meal since Alfred's death. Peter, Wilfred and John provided good company. They all tried as much as possible to avoid discussing the recent bereavement.

"When do you leave for Black River?" Pastor McIntosh asked Peter.

"As soon as I finish business here."

"As you are on that subject, we can plan a time for that," Lynda interjected.

"Whenever you're ready is fine with me."

Anita wished the time for that would come and go quickly. She wasn't expecting anything in that will. Alfred had indicated indirectly, several times, that she wouldn't be a part of that will. Of course, that was during the time when his anger over her relationship with Jerome was at an all time high. On the other hand, John's ear was ticking with excitement. He was bubbling with confidence that something was in that will for him. There was no way he could be left out, he construed.

"We could do it tomorrow?" Lynda said, looking at Anita with an expression as if she was seeking approval from her.

Anita didn't answer. She preferred not to because of her uncertainty about the contents of the will.

"We can," Peter said.

The talk, moving from will to politics, lingered for about another hour. John was unusually happy throughout the chatter, something that didn't go unnoticed by Anita. Was he that thrilled with Elizabeth, or was he over enthusiastic about the possible good news tomorrow might bring?

John was the first to rise the next morning. Peter had informed him before he went off last night that he should be present at the reading of the will. Although he gave no reason, John took it to mean he was a part of it, and rightly so, because the first name to be called at the reading was John's. Alfred had expressed his sincere thanks to John for being a loyal and hardworking overseer. For that, John should remain as overseer for as long as he wanted. Furthermore, he was bequeathed with two acres of land on the northern section of the plantation, and a cash gift of fifty pounds.

Anita and Lynda remained silent and expressionless. To the surprise of everyone, the Yardley Chase Baptist Church was also given fifty pounds. A faint smile moved over Anita's face when she heard it. Pastor McIntosh bowed his head in gratitude.

"My loving and dedicated wife," Peter continued, "shall be in charge of my entire estate until she dies. My brother Jack, who passed on this estate to me, stipulated that it should never be sold, rather it should be passed on to succeeding generations. Therefore, my only daughter Anita, who I love very much, is the heiress to this estate. If Lynda survives Anita, the heir to the estate shall be Andrew, my grandson, whom I expect will pass it on to his children and so on."

Anita and Andrew also received half of his savings in cash, while Lynda received the other half. Anita had become a wealthy woman. She didn't know what to expect, yet here she was proving for herself how much her father truly loved her, despite their strained relationship. Lynda knew all along what was in the will but promised Alfred never to disclose to Anita the contents.

Peter mentioned some personal belongings that were divided up between the maids and some loyal laborers, who had been with him for many years.

"That was the last will and testimony of Alfred Campbell. As the executor of this will, I'm happy to have presented this to you on behalf of the deceased, Alfred Campbell. He was one of the kindest men I have ever met," he added.

"Thank you, Peter," Lynda said. "I guess it will be my turn next to draft that will."

"Thanks, Peter," Anita said.

"Thank you, sir," John said, obviously pleased over his inheritance. John wasn't kin and Alfred was rather kind-hearted to have involved him. Whatever he had given him should be certainly appreciated, John admitted. There were days gone by when he was wishing for the whole estate. The reality that Alfred had a daughter and grandson sent him a message. No matter how much their relationship had been strained, a lone child was something hard to give up on.

"My job is done. It's time to leave," Peter told Anita while they walked out to the stable. Anita thought they were going for a ride. Surprisingly, Peter had already packed.

"I thought you were going to hang on for a few days."

"I would like to do that. I left the office in such a rush that there's a lot of work to catch up on. I'll be back soon," he said, holding Anita's hand and squeezing it.

"I'll miss you. Your company has been great and very much appreciated."

"You really mean that?"

"I do, Peter," Anita said, nodding in approval.

"You'll survive. You're a survivor."

"I'll have to...Dad believed in me. He wanted me to, I cannot let him down. Look at this," she said, making a semi-circle with her hand, "one day it will be mine and I'll have to manage it."

"You'll need a husband, Anita...remember, I'm here."

Anita paused for a moment and looked up at him towering over her. "You would make a nice husband, Peter. Please forgive me...now more than ever I need some more time to think...to sort out my life."

"I understand, Anita...please don't get me wrong. I'm in no rush. It was only a reminder because I don't want to lose you." Peter's hands went on her shoulders; Anita knew he was sincere.

"That's what I like about you, Peter. You're very understanding and honest."

"Thanks. That means a lot to me. Maybe one day you should come to Black River for a week to get away from here."

"Maybe I should. At least you give me something to think about. When will you come again?"

"Whenever you want me to I will." He grinned widely.

"I don't want to take you away from your work. Whenever you've cleared your backlog, I'll be there."

Lynda came out to join them.

"It's sad to see you go, Peter, although I know you must," she said, handing him a packaged lunch.

"Thanks. I hate to see what my desk will be like tomorrow."

"Don't you worry, you'll make it," Anita said.

"I would imagine we won't be seeing you in these parts for a while," Lynda remarked.

"I was just telling Anita here that I'd be seeing her soon."

Lynda welcomed that idea. "Oh! That's nice of you."

"I should be going."

Peter planted a kiss on Anita's forehead and one on Lynda's cheek. He mounted his horse and rode out of Jack's Place reluctantly. He wished he could have stayed a few more days.

A thought ran in his head when Peter approached the

crossroad: one leading to Black River and the other to Top Hill. *Leonora!* Should he stop to say a quick goodbye? She was only about ten minutes up the road.

Peter found Leonora preparing a flower garden in front of the house. She dropped everything she was doing as soon as she laid eyes on him coming through the gate.

"Isn't this a surprise?" she said, almost running to meet him. Leonora's dirty hands barely touched Peter on both arms as she tipped in order to kiss him on his cheek.

"I can see you're happy to see me," he said, startled by her reaction.

"I am. I thought you were going to leave without seeing me."

"I was going to do that. When I reached at the intersection there I thought I had to stop."

"That was nice of you, Peter. You've made my day."

"How's your father?"

"He's inside with a patient." She smiled, obviously pleased with that.

"He's getting busy."

"We cannot complain. There have been a few people coming by as word gets around that a doctor is in Yardley Chase. How's Anita doing?"

"She's fine. She's a strong woman with a survival instinct."

"You like her?"

That question had to come sooner rather than later. "Who wouldn't like Anita? She's the type of person who gets along with everyone she meets," Peter said, trying to be as honest as possible with his answer.

"Is she seeing anyone?"

"Hmmm, I doubt that. Then again one cannot be too certain."

They walked over to a tree nearby to sit on a wooden bench. "How come she has stayed single all these years?"

"That's a long story. I wouldn't have time to go into all of that today."

"Story? Did something happen to her?"

"You see that beautiful cliff over there?" Peter indicated with his hand.

"Lover's Leap?"

"Have you ever gone there?"

"I did one day last week. I couldn't believe a place on earth could look like that. It's spectacular."

"Good. The name Lover's Leap came a few years ago."

"How? Tell me. It doesn't make sense you start and you cannot finish the story."

Peter paused to rub his jaw. He looked up into the sky, the sun glaring at him. The morning was getting older. He should've been in Southfield already.

"To make a long story short, Anita was in love with a slave. The slave, in turn, was in love with another slave. When the secret affair came out into the light, all hell broke loose. Their love couldn't remain a secret forever. The slaves eventually jumped from the cliff, rather than live without each other."

"Anita was left out of the picture?" a curious Leonora asked.

"Her father vowed that if she didn't leave him, the slave would be sold. Anita had planned to run away with him not knowing that Jerome was seeing another slave. When Alfred found the two slaves at their secret meeting place at Lookout, the name it had first, the slaves probably thought they would either be sold or killed. They didn't like either option; the only alternative was to jump. Anita loved him to death and didn't care. Eight months later she had a baby for him."

Leonora placed her hand over her mouth in fright. "A baby? She was that serious about him? Where's he now?" Leonora turned around to face him.

"Andrew left for Kingston last week. He's one bright young man whose ambition is to go into politics."

"He's a mulatto?"

"A very, very bright one, too. He's an addition to the growing number of them speaking with one voice on behalf of ex-slaves."

"Hmmm, Anita is proving to be an interesting individual. I must admit I underestimated her."

Peter rose to his feet. "This has to be a short visit. I must go…"

"I realize that," she said, rising, too. "When will you come again?"

"I don't know, some time soon."

"I may well come to Black River to be near you at least for a week, if Anita doesn't mind of course," she teased.

"Leonora? You talk as if Anita and I have something going?" Peter said.

"You don't?"

Before he answered, Peter drew her to him quickly and kissed her on the mouth. She didn't resist; instead Leonora assisted him in the way he chose to answer.

Torrential rainfall scoured Yardley Chase for the rest of the week. On Tuesday afternoon, the clouds spread their wings over the entire sky. The crawling pillars of cumulus and nimbus clouds gobbled up quickly the few remaining patches of blue. An unusual darkness crept over the land, sending birds quickly to their nests, humans to their houses. Horses were sent into their stables, while a few of the cows, sheep and goats remained in the green pastures.

The rains came with a vengeance, pounding rooftops with hail at first, then powerful drops that seemed to want to penetrate whatever they were hitting. The rains started around four o' clock and fell intermittently until Saturday morning. The southern portion of the island was mostly affected by the rainy weather.

A few farmers lost some goats and sheep at the end of it all. Crops, mainly kidney beans, corn, and tomatoes were washed away.

The calm came at midday. Anita was relieved that it was all over. Lush greenery was all around the district. The birds were happy, too, that the rains had given them a break. The sky was dotted with all species.

Anita slept most of the time for the nearly five days indoors, trying to catch up on lost sleep over the past few weeks. She read the Bible and prayed, at times often using the opportunity to discuss with Lynda the future of Jack's Place. They agreed on diversification, rather than cultivating more sugar cane; the plantation would try to benefit from an ever-expanding tobacco market.

Anita saw the void in Lynda's life left by the passing of Alfred. She tried as best as she could to cheer her up, even suggesting they take a trip somewhere. They could go to Kingston, to look for Andrew. Lynda agreed to go some time.

Lynda decided to bring up a subject that had been weighing heavily on her mind over dinner Saturday afternoon. The time was here; precious time had been moving on slowly but surely, she thought.

"How are you and Peter getting on these days? I'm curious to know whether there's a relationship. Not intruding—only out of curiosity," she said tactfully.

"Hmm. I'm not in the least surprised you ask," Anita responded.

"How come?"

"Well, let's face it. Peter is an eligible bachelor. I'm single, and on top of that he has been visiting regularly nowadays. Who wouldn't think something must be going on?"

"Is there something going on?" Lynda asked, sipping her tea.

"Not really. Peter likes me, I know that."

"And?"

"I told him I need a little more time. That was shortly before I went to Kingston. Dad's death came. I haven't been thinking about him since," Anita said, being even more suspicious that Lynda was pushing Peter.

"This could be the perfect opportunity to try to have the security of a husband. We're all getting old, Anita." She smiled, not wanting to sound too domineering.

"I know, Mom, I know. I want to make sure there's no mistake about the man I'll marry."

"I agree with you on that. I've no reservation about Peter."

"You like him that much?"

"I do. We've known him for a while. I know he could make a good husband."

"How did Dad feel about him?" Anita asked, putting her mother on the spot. Anita's past with Jerome would somehow have been discussed in any talk about her future. It was a subject Lynda wouldn't want to revisit again.

"Your dad thought very highly of Peter. He trusted him one hundred percent with his affairs. That was the business part of it. On the social side, I remember he said once that he wished he had a daughter who was interested in Peter," Lynda said, her hand on her chin.

"Hmmm, well who can tell, he could be the one for me. I guess we'll all have to wait to see."

Anita could barely wait to go to church the next morning. Wilfred was on her mind all week and last night, following that conversation she had with her mother.

Wilfred was standing at the front door greeting members and visitors.

"I was hoping you wouldn't get washed away." Wilfred grinned. "How's your mom?"

"She's fine, thought of coming out today but had to catch up on a few things."

"Glad you could make it. What a wonderful blessing we got this week. Even though some farmers suffered losses, I'm certain many are smiling this morning—the crops, too. It's a good day to give thanks to God."

"Indeed, it's a good day, Pastor," Leonora said from behind. Wilfred and Anita didn't see her coming up behind; her utterance frightened them.

"Oh! Where did you come from?" Anita asked, looking over her shoulder at Leonora.

"Out of the blue," she quipped.

"It's good to see you again," Pastor McIntosh said.

"I'm happy to be here."

A couple came up behind Leonora and she stepped inside the church. Anita was ahead of Leonora. She was thinking of waiting for her as both of them could sit beside each other. However, Anita changed her mind.

The service was one of thanksgiving to God for the showers from above. It went a few minutes beyond the usual time to accommodate some baptisms.

"I would imagine I should be thinking about that, too," Anita told Wilfred after the service.

His eyes search hers and Wilfred appeared pleased. "It's something every human being should think about. In the fullness of time, it will be the most important step anyone will ever make in their lifetime—giving their heart to the Lord."

"You're right, Pastor, you're right. I know those two people, who were baptized a while ago, must feel like a burden has been removed from their shoulders."

"There's no doubt about that. That's precisely what happens."

Leonora waltzed her way up to them again. Anita was annoyed this time. She recounted that it had been quite a few times that Leonora had walked in on their conversation.

"That was a good sermon, Pastor, a really good sermon. The whole of Yardley Chase should have heard it."

"Thanks, Miss Simmonds. I appreciate it but the thanks must go to the Almighty who gives the inspiration."

"Don't you agree it was most inspiring, Anita?"

"Of course I do."

"My dad will soon start coming out regularly. I hope he does because he's missing a lot," Leonora said.

"That would be good. Please encourage him to come out."

"You should come over one night for dinner and both of you can talk," she suggested.

Anita was convinced Leonora was extending that invitation maliciously. She wanted to see her reaction. A smart, wise Anita chose to remain calm. She was pretending she either heard the invitation and it meant nothing, or she didn't hear at all.

"That sounds good. I'll have to reorganize my schedule. I'll let you know soon. I expect a pastoral team from Kingston here in a few days. I know that I'll be very busy," Pastor McIntosh said.

"As long as I know you're coming I'm willing to wait." She giggled.

"By the way, I believe Elizabeth is coming with the team. Remember you met her in Kingston," Pastor McIntosh said, turning her attention to Anita.

"Oh! I remember her. Where will she be staying? If you want, she could stay by me," Anita offered, using the opportunity to shut Leonora out of the conversation.

"That would be nice of you, Anita. I'm positive she would like that."

"If you need any extra space for the team, we have a spare room," Leonora said, working her way back into the conversation.

"Thanks, Leonora, I'll let you know as soon as the team gets here."

"Oh, you're welcome."

"I'm looking forward to the visit. I'm trying my utmost best to ensure they have an enjoyable stay."

"One more thing, do prepare to have a long evening whenever you come for dinner. When my father starts he won't stop," Leonora hinted.

"Don't worry, I can handle that."

"See you soon," she smiled, "and, Anita, do enjoy the rest of your conversation."

Anita said nothing. *Happy riddance*, she thought.

John Stewart had some time to think—to think about his most serious challenge in life: the challenge to find a wife. His good master Alfred had left him some prime land, a reasonable amount of cash, and the security of a job till his retirement. The only thing he needed was a woman.

The letter John had in his hand could provide the answer. Elizabeth, whom he had met at the Baptist Mission in Kingston, had written to him. Her letter informed John she was on her way to visit Yardley Chase. By the time John would receive the mail via Pastor McIntosh, she would have left Kingston with a pastoral team that would be visiting the parishes of Manchester and St. Elizabeth.

John concluded Elizabeth was interested in him. They had a very long talk in Kingston. She showed interest in knowing more about him. Since then, John hadn't been thinking about Anita. In fact, he was indebted to Anita for introducing Elizabeth to him because she could jolly well be the woman who could change his miserable, lonely, and hopeless life.

John was sitting on his verandah when Anita passed by on her way from church. He was so deep in dreamland that she almost slipped by without John seeing her.

"Hi there!" he shouted.

"Oh! Hi, John! How are you doing? Are you alright?"

"I'm fine. How about you?"

John rose from the chair. He walked out to the gate where she had stopped. Anita made no attempt to come inside. John opened the gate and slipped outside to meet her.

"You look very happy...that smile won't leave your face. I saw it from way back there. Am I missing something here?" Anita teased.

"Hmmm, it's Elizabeth." He laughed, almost aloud.

"She's coming to Yardley Chase."

"Yes, how did you know that?"

"I heard a few minutes ago from Pastor McIntosh."

"Oh! I'm glad, Anita. She's a wonderful woman."

"It's good you can say that after only meeting her once."

"She is...believe me, she is...I almost can't wait to see her," John said eagerly.

"Do you think you may be the reason for her coming?" Anita smiled.

"I would hope so. Even if that's not the case, I'm thrilled she's going to be here. Where will she be staying?"

"I've offered to put her up."

"Great! This means she'll be nearby."

"As near as can be, John. You couldn't have wanted her nearer," she joked.

"You're making me blush, Anita."

"Could be deliberate. I take it you'll have to start thinking about coming to church."

John was silent. Anita could see he wasn't thinking about that. "Well, you caught me on that one. Never thought of it y'know."

"You'll have to, John," she said, trapping him with that likelihood.

"If it means that, I'll be there. Church, here I come!" John said aloud, apparently recovering from the jolt.

"That's the way to go, John. Nevertheless, I must warn you that you shouldn't be thinking about going to church only because a woman you like is going to be there."

John peered at her from beneath his eyes. "I agree with you wholeheartedly, my dear," he said, scratching his unruly beard. "I can only hope some of the young women in this district aren't going to church because of Pastor," he said jokingly.

That statement could have been meant for Anita...or Leonora. However, Anita assumed John didn't know of her feelings for Pastor. He could only be speculating or trying to see her reaction. After all, Anita knew John had never given up on her.

"I hope so, too, John. The church isn't any place. It's a holy assembly as commanded by the living God. It's to praise not to satisfy our own egos and emotions," she said confidently.

"I hope you're right, Anita. I don't pretend to be righteous as some people do. I'm a sinner."

"I am, too. See you, John, I have to go."

"See you tomorrow, Anita. We'll have a busy week after all those rains."

"That's right. You have a productive week. Remember, don't you think too much now about Elizabeth." She smiled as she walked away.

"Maybe I will, maybe I won't. At least I have someone to think about," he said triumphantly, somewhat puzzled about Anita's sudden departure.

Did his comments about church-going offend her? That was the only likely explanation for her abrupt move. If Anita was capable of keeping her love affair with Jerome very secretive, she was also likely to be covering up her reasons for going to church, as well as her admiration for the young and handsome Pastor.

Peter was another possibility. John had been busy, and couldn't find any time to observe what had been going on, if anything, during his recent visits. Could his trips to Yardley Chase be more than business?

John's obsession with Anita's life could only prove that he hadn't gotten over her. He tried to tell himself many times that he had to get her out of his thoughts as soon as possible. The easiest way to do that would be to find another woman. Elizabeth? Her visit couldn't have been timelier. John roared with laughter inside, a groaning sound vibrating under his breath. The husky laughter even produced the presence of tobacco smell on his breath. The time was overdue; he should have had a woman in his life already. As a habit, John was about to beat his chest in triumph but decided to wait until Elizabeth arrived.

Elizabeth, accompanied by three young pastors-in-training, trotted into Yardley Chase Friday afternoon. A tired bunch, they could barely wait to be seated in Wilfred's couch. Nevertheless, their voice rang with excitement that they had finally arrived in southern Jamaica.

Pastor McIntosh offered them a drink, explaining that dinner would be served at Jack's Place. Anita had extended the invitation to the team to have their meals there while they were in Yardley Chase. She felt much obliged that the Mission in Kingston was taking care of Andrew. Anita wanted to extend her gratitude. Pastor McIntosh was very pleased with her gesture because it would save him a lot of time to organize meals.

Elizabeth was also very happy she would be staying with Anita. During the short stay in Kingston, she and Anita had established a good friendship.

Anita had been expecting them Friday afternoon. As the light of day began to fade at sunset, Anita was disappointed that they weren't there yet. The meal was prepared and waiting. A knock on the front door interrupted her thoughts. The sweaty palms of her hands curled around the knob of the door and pulled it to her.

The beefy face of John greeted her. Anita didn't have to guess why he was there.

"Evening, is she here yet?" John asked excitedly.

"Good evening, John. When I heard the door knock, I was hoping it was them."

"I wonder if something happened."

"Are they here?" Lynda shouted to Anita from upstairs.

"No, Mom."

"I should take a walk up to Pastor McIntosh. They could be there," John suggested, looking behind him. "Do you want to come?"

"Of course, I'm anxious to hear from Andrew as you are full of anxiety to see Elizabeth."

"Heh! Heh Heh! You're right on that one."

Anita closed the door behind her, not bothering to inform her mother. As they were about to go through the gate, a walking party of five people forced them to stop. Even though it was almost dark, Anita recognized Wilfred's voice. The party came into view. She was right.

"Hey, look who's here!" Pastor McIntosh said. "We're no strangers, we've all met already, right?"

"Yes," Anita said, remembering the three men she had met around the lunch table while she was at the Mission in Kingston.

Elizabeth was glad to see her. She came up to hug her, patting Anita on the back as she did. "Boy, am I glad to see you."

"I am, too."

Elizabeth released her quickly to reach out to shake John's hand. "It's good to see you, too, John."

"I'm delighted," John beamed.

"We're all hungry, let's go eat. There'll be lots of time to talk," Pastor McIntosh said. They all agreed.

An hour later, Jack's Place was echoing with laughter. Stomachs that were yearning for food a short time ago, were filled. The chairs around Lynda's huge dining table were all occupied—something that didn't occur very often at Jack's Place. Lynda liked the company. She was also pleased that all the food that had been prepared was gone.

John sat next to Elizabeth, while Anita was seated between her mother and Pastor McIntosh. The three pastors-in-training, Byron Burns, Clinton Reid, and Alton Wellington, sat next to each other. They appeared to be in their mid thirties. Articulate and knowledgeable in history, politics and the Bible, they were well versed in their arguments.

Anita had never enjoyed herself that much in a long time. She hardly said anything during the conversation, preferring to listen and learn from these well-educated men. Pastor Wellington had given her a letter from Andrew. Anita wanted to read it but didn't get the opportunity to do that. She was quite aware that her guests had to be taken care of first.

"Andrew is going to make a good politician, Miss Campbell. I must say he has impressed many people in Kingston. Last week, he toured the House of Assembly and insists he will be sitting in there one day as an elected official," Pastor Wellington said.

"Yardley Chase is proud of him. We're confident he will, too," Anita remarked.

"He'll be a future leader in whichever capacity he chooses," Pastor McIntosh said.

"It was my husband's last wish that we give him whatever help he needs to get there. We pledged to do that. We're proud of him," Lynda said, smiling warmly.

"Andrew realizes the plight of former slaves. He knows that even with Crown Colonies or whatever system of government Britain uses, these poor people have a far way to go to achieve anything. Socially, there's much to be desired; that's another whole problem in itself. Poverty, jobs, housing, are very serious problems. Jamaica needs men like Andrew. We here in Yardley Chase hope our small district will produce one such leader," Pastor McIntosh said.

They all agreed. With the agreement came the salutations, accolades for a good meal and a very entertaining evening.

After they had gone, Anita sat around the table with Lynda. She started to read aloud the letter from her son. Elizabeth looked on, while John prepared to listen attentively.

Dear Mom,

I am hoping all is well with you and Grandma.

I am sorry to hear about Grandfather's death. It came as a shock to me and I have to admit I went into mourning for the entire week after I got the news.

One of my fervent wishes was to have spent more time with him—to get to know him better. However, I am somewhat relieved that he had pledged to do all the best for me. With his help, I know I am much more comfortable here. May his soul rest in peace.

The Baptist Mission has been very good to me. I have no complaints whatsoever. People here speak very highly of Pastor McIntosh and this has assisted me a great deal. Please give him my regards.

I have started some classes in politics and history. I have even witnessed some protests here recently. Undoubtedly, this makes the classes even more interesting.

Mama, I must admit I miss you badly, very badly. At nights, I have bad dreams about being harmed and you weren't around to help. I believe you must get them, too.

Anyway, back to reality. Kingston is busy but very nice, a stark contrast to Yardley Chase. There are many places to go and people to meet. I'm glad I came here, Mama. I wish you were here, though. I often think about my father and I know deep down within that I must do what I have to do. By so doing, I will bring some honor to him for being the son of a slave.

I love you, Mama. Tell Grandma I love her, too. I am hoping I will be down for Christmas. Please pray for me. I go to church every Sunday. I feel a lot closer to God now. I thank Him for that. Give my regards to Pastor McIntosh, John, Simon, Jerry and Sally and all the workers on the plantation.

I am longing to see you write. Please send a letter with the team. Love you, Mama.

Your only Son,
Andrew.

P.S. Tell John to take good care of Teddy.

Anita clutched the letter to her chest with tears in her eyes. "What a sweet letter, Mom?"

"It is, my dear. We must plan to visit him soon. You should ask Peter if he would like to go to Kingston with us, along with John here," Lynda suggested.

"I'm ready anytime you are," a smiling John said, looking at Elizabeth. She returned the smile in a way that suggested she thought it would be a good idea.

Anita thought about that for a while. Pastor McIntosh would have been better. How would she get around this one?

"We can ask him, although I doubt if he would go."

"Why?" Lynda asked, stirring the sugar in her tea.

"He told me he has a lot of work to catch up on."

"We wouldn't ask him now. Give him a few months."

Anita suspected it would be pretty difficult to find another excuse not to invite Peter. She had to start thinking fast.

"Who's Peter?" Elizabeth asked.

"He's our barrister," Lynda replied.

"Well, I think it would be a good idea if you all come to spend a whole week. Andrew would be delighted. It could be a welcome break from Yardley Chase. I'm certain Wilfred would come along, too," Elizabeth said, looking at Anita.

Anita's face glowed in the light. Elizabeth saw her reaction. She guessed she was pleased with that latter statement. However, little did she know that what she had done was to add more confusion to Anita's state of mind. Anita wanted Wilfred to go, not Peter. The two of them would be too much to handle.

"We'll see how it goes," Anita said. "I think we should get some sleep. It's getting late."

John rose from his comfortable seat. "I wish you all have a good night. I'll see you tomorrow."

Elizabeth came up to him, patting him on the shoulder. "Good night, John. Thanks for coming."

Anita took Elizabeth to her room across the hallway from hers. Lynda appeared to be tired and retired to her room.

"Hmmm, this is nice," Elizabeth said, referring to her room.

"It's pretty comfortable. I hope you'll find it that way."

"Come on, Anita, this is like a palace! I feel I could live here all my life."

"With John?"

Elizabeth stared at Anita. "John! Hmm..."

"Not possible?"

"It is possible but..."

"But what! John is a nice man. He needs someone...like you."

"Just like how Wilfred needs a nice woman...like you."

Anita blushed. "I would imagine both of us have waited on that four-letter word—time."

"You said it right."

CHAPTER 10

The time went by quickly and Sunday morning caught Anita unaware. She took Elizabeth riding around Yardley Chase all day Saturday; a great deal of time was spent at Lover's Leap. Anita traced the history there, revealing to Elizabeth that it got the name because of what happened to Andrew's father and another slave. Anita also told her about the affair with Jerome, and her subsequent lengthy struggle to get over a broken heart.

Elizabeth was fascinated with the beauty of the cliff. She kept peering down and out into the turquoise waters of the Caribbean Sea, as well as at the mountains descending into the sea. Elizabeth never dreamed such a place could exist in these remote parts. No wonder it was once a haven for young lovers. In the future it could very well be that place again.

Elizabeth was looking forward to church. She had never attended a rural church service before.

As adherents to the faith trickled in, one thing was obvious to her. The people were well dressed; church was a very important part of their lives. She assumed that, given the fact that there weren't many activities around, unlike in Kingston. The church was their life.

Leonora was one of the first persons who caught Elizabeth's eyes. Her style of dressing was an attention grabber. She must have landed from England yesterday, Elizabeth concluded. Her embroidered lilac dress with bonnet to match was noticeable to the eyes of male and female, middle-aged and elderly.

"Who is that woman?" Elizabeth asked Anita, who was sitting beside her three rows from the front seat—Leonora's usual position.

"She's Leonora, the daughter of the district's doctor who came from England a few weeks ago."

"I was wondering when she arrived."

"She has never dressed like this before. I wonder why."

"Maybe that's the reason," Elizabeth hinted. Pastor McIntosh was introducing Leonora to the three pastors-in-training.

"She knew they were coming. That woman is something else," Anita remarked, nodding her head in disgust.

"What do you mean?"

"She has been after all the eligible bachelors around here."

"Like who."

"Pastor McIntosh...Peter."

"John?"

Anita smiled, almost laughing. "John doesn't come to church. I don't believe she has met him."

"She may meet him today. John told me he's coming even if he's late."

"She has been a thorn in my side ever since she came here."

"Isn't there anything you can do about her?"

Anita looked surprised. "My dear, I don't have a clue. Any ideas?"

"Enter the competition," Elizabeth said dryly.

Anita couldn't answer her right away. The organ began to play the first hymn, as soon as she was about to answer.

Pastor McIntosh had an attentive audience as usual. He spoke longer than normal because of his guests from the headquarters, in Kingston.

Leonora was at it again after service. This time, it was with Clinton Reid, one of the visiting pastors. She cornered him minutes after church was dismissed.

"We're so happy to have you here," Leonora told him.

Clinton, who was about six feet two, looked down on her admiringly.

"We're happy to be here to meet such friendly people. I like it here," he said, looking around the room, "all relaxed and quiet."

"I'd like to have you all over for dinner one evening. My father is the doctor here."

"Oh! That would be nice."

"Do you know where you'll be stationed in the future?" Leonora asked, leaning her head to one side.

"As a matter of fact, I could well be in these parts. There's a church going up in the Pedro Plains area, Flagaman to be exact. I could end up there."

"Where's that?"

"Go outside, look to the west, you can see part of the Plains."

"Uh-huh, I've seen that flat piece of land down there. I'm always staring at it from my window. It's beautiful."

"We're going down there later in the week. From there we go to Black River, the final leg of our trip."

"Will Pastor McIntosh be coming with you?" Leonora asked.

"He had indicated an interest in going. I don't know if he has decided."

"I've been planning to go to Black River for the longest while to try to find a job there, but I haven't been able to; maybe I should use this opportunity to go."

Clinton didn't read into her intentions. Had he known that Leonora's sole intent was to get closer to Pastor McIntosh, or any young man for that matter, he would have discouraged her from going.

"We've space for about three people." He grinned.

"Well, thanks for the invitation. We'll see."

The crowd started to dissipate after a while. Anita said goodbye to a few people before she headed for the door. John, who came late, was busy escorting Elizabeth around introducing her to all and sundry. Anita had decided she would leave them. She felt lonely with no one to talk to; she decided to leave. Pastor McIntosh walked up in time to block her path. He did it in a very comical way, skipping into her path then hopping back out of it. She hadn't seen him coming; nevertheless, when the pastor stood in front of her laughing, Anita found it amusing. Some people standing nearby looked in wonderment trying to determine the source of her laughter. They could only see the pastor standing in front of her. They were baffled.

"What's so funny?" Pastor McIntosh said, feeling embarrassed. "Can you please share the joke?"

Anita started to laugh again. "I...I never...I never imagined you could be so comical. You look so funny. Were you ever in the theater?"

"No. I thought I would cheer you up. You look sad. I couldn't let you go like that."

Anita's eyes darted into his face. Those words were good to hear. "Thanks for your concern. I'm a wee tired...thought I'd go to get some rest."

"I was going to ask you...but it's all right...you're tired," he said, walking her to the door.

"Go ahead," Anita said, anxious to hear the rest of the question. How could she not hear what he was about to ask her.

"Are you up to a journey?"

"Journey? What journey?"

"Not as long as Kingston, maybe about forty miles both ways. Byron has asked me to accompany them to the Pedro Plains and Black River to look at some churches there. One of them may be posted there soon."

"Hmmm, Black River. That sounds nice. I haven't been there for many years."

"I haven't been there. I know Elizabeth wouldn't mind your company at all."

"Elizabeth? How about you? Aren't you the one inviting me?" At first, Anita wished he could take back the question. She never meant to ask it. It was too late. She waited for his reaction.

Wilfred's reaction was one of indifference. If he was reading something into it, his expression said nothing of such. It was one of those characteristics he had that Anita wished she could understand more, i.e. he rarely showed any emotions to situations where she would have loved to see his true reaction. Could her conclusion be wrong? Perhaps his duty as a pastor required him to act responsibly in all situations. That part of him Anita might never know, she feared.

"Of course, I'm inviting you," he said in a sturdy voice. "I thought the break from here would do you some good. It could be tiring, yes. It could also be refreshing."

"You know what, I'm in on it. When do you leave?"

"Wednesday morning, bright and early."

"I'll be there. I agree that such a journey could be good for me. It's not long. I'm in good company, very good company. I can even drop in on Peter."

"There you go. As you mentioned his name, how are you two getting along?"

Anita didn't know how to answer. "Peter is a very nice person. I find him easy to get along with."

"He's a nice young man. I was wondering how he has stayed single for so long."

"Good question, wrong person to ask." She smiled. By this time, they had reached outside on the lawn where a few others were enjoying the bright sunshine.

"Hmmm, it's not my business anyway," he said, scratching his chin.

"Why did you ask anyway?"

"Curiosity."

"Are you certain there's nothing more to it?" Anita felt herself getting very brave with the questions. Why not, the opportunities were there to ask them, she contemplated.

Wilfred turned to look at her during the walk to the gate. "Quite certain."

"Okay, I trust you on that. I think I may know why. I could be wrong, though."

"I'm listening."

"Peter wants to marry me."

Wilfred hesitated before he answered. It was at that moment Anita knew her answer had an effect on him. One thing she knew about him for sure: Wilfred answered readily to almost anything that was asked. Anita had started to notice that. The only time he hesitated to answer was when he was surprised by the information given to him.

"Interesting. Do you want to marry him?" The words barely came out of his mouth.

"I've been thinking. I told him I needed time." Anita hoped that would get him jealous, if he had any thoughts about her at all.

"Is there a likelihood of a positive answer?" Wilfred asked, running his fingers along the corners of his mouth.

"There could be. As I said, Peter is a nice man. I'm getting older each day, and I no longer have a father. I need someone to lean on...don't have much time."

"One has to be careful, especially someone in your position, Anita."

"What do you mean?"

"You're a rich woman."

"I have thought about that, too. Peter knew me from before I was rich. He was crazy about me from his very first trip here." She wanted to be certain the message she was sending to Wilfred was getting home. The message: was he interested in her? Anita could sense that he didn't want her to leave.

"That may be so. What would make you change your mind?" Wilfred asked grudgingly.

"God can."

"How?"

"I would prefer to marry someone who's getting to know God the way I'm doing, or someone who knows him already and is living the Christian way."

"Huh, very interesting," he said, his face showing cheerfulness. Obviously, he was pleased with that answer.

"I need a nice Christian man. I'm convinced about that more and more every day."

"Our God is a God of miracles and he can change anything, Anita. I'm sorry to keep you so long. Give my regards to Lynda."

"I must say I enjoyed this conversation very much."

"I did, too."

When Teddy echoed his crow at daybreak Wednesday morning, Anita slipped out of bed to prepare for her journey to Black River. Elizabeth heard her movements and joined her.

Since Sunday, Anita had been living on the memory of her last conversation with Pastor McIntosh. Elizabeth had also informed her of a growing friendship with John. Anita's own preoccupation with Wilfred didn't drive home the point about John finally getting someone interested in him. It was only last night the conversation came up again. Anita truly understood and began to encourage Elizabeth to stay close to John because he was a good man for her.

John was already in the stables getting the buggy ready for Anita and Elizabeth, even before they knew it. As far as Anita knew, John wasn't slated to go. But when she saw him up that early getting everything ready, Anita knew he had every intention of going.

A vast stretch of flat land sprawling along the southwestern section of the parish of St. Elizabeth was what made up the Pedro Plains. The small fishing village of Great Bay was the newest location for a church. Pastor McIntosh and his team were very encouraged by the growth in attendance there. The community needed a shepherd at the earliest possible time. They only spent a day there; the next morning, Friday, they left for the biggest town in the parish—Black River.

Anita was enjoying the journey. She chatted with Elizabeth most of the time. They used two buggies, one for the pastors, the other for the two women and John. Anita had been hoping Pastor McIntosh would have joined them but protocol dictated that he be with his guests. She was rather anxious to reach Black River where she would be able to talk with him. This was Peter's town, so to speak, hence it would be interesting to see what would happen when he came into the picture.

Back In Yardley Chase, Leonora Simmonds had been very miserable from the moment she confirmed that Pastor McIntosh went to Black River with the team. Anita's presence added to her misery.

Early Friday morning, on her way to market, she extended the journey to include a stop at the church. Sally was the only one around. Leonora was glad to be filled in on what had been happening.

"You seem to know a lot, Sally."

"I'm 'round here all di time, ma'am, mi know somet'ings." She grinned, eyes sparkling in the early morning sunlight.

"I think you could be more useful around here."

"Sure, ma'am."

"I don't think you know exactly what I mean, Sally," Leonora said, dismounting from her horse.

"What, ma'am?" The smile left her face, indicating that she had picked up her line of reasoning.

"I could give you some money if you keep a very sharp eye on what goes along around here. I mean with the pastor...his friends y'know."

"Friends, ma'am? Everybody is a friend."

"I know that. But some may want to be closer than friends."

"Like who, ma'am?" she asked pretentiously.

Leonora came closer, speaking softer the nearer she got to Sally. "You don't know?"

Sally looked down on her toes, rubbing them in the brown loose dirt on the pathway leading up to the manse. "I don't t'ink a know anyt'ing, ma'am," Sally said abruptly.

"You don't think you know? Suppose I give you a shilling if you can tell me who's the woman that visits him more often. Each time you are able to tell me when she visits, how long they spend together, where they spend it, I'll give you a penny. And here's the bonus; if you can tell me what they did, I'll add a farthing on that."

Sally's eyes rolled out of her head. That was a lot of money. She looked at her in bewilderment. Where did this woman come from? What was she up to? What did she plan to do with all that information? "As I said, I know somet'ings, ma'am. No woman eva come here," she replied, wondering if she should lie to get the money.

"You're certain about that, Sally?"

"Yes, ma'am."

"Well, well I find that very hard to believe. Maybe the person came and you didn't see."

"Hmmm maybe, ma'am. Who's dis person, ma'am?"

"Anita."

"Miss Anita, ma'am?" Sally said, unmistakenly surprised. "Miss Anita don't come here, ma'am. If she come, these eyes neva saw her."

"Hmm, strange indeed," she said, hoping she had heard her correctly. Leonora wasn't that familiar with the dialect, although she could understand Sally.

"But what she would be doing here, ma'am?"

"That is what you must find out, Sally. Remember, the pay is good."

"It is, ma'am, sure is good," Sally giggled.

Black River seemed like a quiet, little town. The Black River, after which it was named, appeared black as it flowed along the eastern side of the town out into the blue sea.

The pastors as well as Elizabeth took a sudden liking to the town. It was very busy when they arrived there Friday afternoon. The two general stores were very busy so was one of the inns where they checked to stay for the weekend.

The crew was worn out by the afternoon journey, as the sun poured out its evening warmth on them. The sun shone directly in their face because they had been traveling west. At the end of it all, most of them had pink faces, except for Anita and John who were used to the heat.

The sunburn added a little discomfort to their tiredness. By nightfall, they were dead tired. Sleep came swiftly, with little time to talk.

The next morning, Peter's maid was about to serve him breakfast on his porch. She was distracted by the burly figure of a man walking around to the back of the house. At first, she thought he was an intruder. Irene Walters, the maid, ran through the kitchen door to the porch to inform Peter before John could reach the back.

Peter tilted his head from the book he was reading to see John coming toward him.

"Hey, look who's here!" Peter said with an outstretched arm.

"Good morning, Peter." The maid went back inside the moment she determined that they knew each other.

"What breeze blow you here?" he joked, beckoning to him to sit down.

"I'm here with Pastor McIntosh, two other pastors, a young lady accompanying them and Anita."

"Anita? Where are they?"

"Over at the Logwood Inn. They are having something to eat."

"Join me for breakfast. When we finish we can go over there." Peter grinned.

"I have something to eat already, though I wouldn't mind a cup of tea."

"When you came in?"

"Yesterday afternoon. We came in from Pedro Plains. We were all so tired that we went straight to bed. "

"Who's the other woman?" Peter asked curiously.

"Elizabeth Cameron...from the Baptist Mission head office. She's a wonderful woman."

"I look forward to meeting her. Who can tell, maybe she likes it down here and would like to stay," Peter said, hinting she could be of interest to him.

"Don't go there, Peter. She's already mine," John assured him.

Peter stopped the fork from going into his mouth. "What? You are kidding me, aren't you?"

"No, not at all."

"If that's so, then you are one quick individual."

"Let's say desperate. You know Anita was my choice. I have lived with that hurt and pain for many years. Now I have to move on. In so doing, I need someone to soothe that pain. I'm convinced that someone is Elizabeth. You may be the one for Anita if you are quick like me."

"Tell me more, John. It seems like there are things I'm missing out on. What's this with Anita and me?"

"You like her, don't you?" John asked, the gulps of coffee rattling down his throat.

"Well, I cannot deny that I do."

"I know you do. I'm not that blind y'know. Have you told her?"

"Of course I do but..."

"But what...she hasn't made up her mind?"

"How did you know that? Have you been speaking with her?" Peter's scrambled eggs were of no more interest to him; the conversation had changed everything. On most of Peter's trips to Yardley Chase, he had never spoken with John that much. In fact, he was often in the field, thereby allowing little time to even have a chat.

"Not really. I know Anita. I know how she thinks. She was the one who sent me here to inform you that we're here. But then, there's the pastor..."

Peter was dumbfounded. "Pastor? Which pastor?"

"Pastor McIntosh?"

"What are you trying to tell me, John?" Peter took a quick sip of coffee to keep the conversation flowing.

"This is only my personal suspicion."

"Of course, you know that suspicion cannot stand in court," Peter teased, trying to trivialize whatever conclusions he might be drawing.

"That's why I emphasize personal suspicion. I have no doubts that Anita is in love with Pastor McIntosh."

"What makes you think so?" Peter asked calmly.

"There are several reasons. She goes to church every Wednesday and Sunday..."

"Nothing is wrong with that."

"If you are serious about God, I agree. However, I don't believe Anita is a convert."

"John, I believe you may be too judgmental there."

"No, Peter, Anita has been searching for true love ever since that slave died. She has had a hard time finding her match. She turned to the church for help. Hmm, there was Pastor McIntosh," he said, flashing his hand like his theory was right.

"Don't you think he's only attending to her spiritual needs?" Peter asked calmly again.

"You know what, I've a funny inclination that the pastor doesn't know about Anita's feelings."

Peter nodded in agreement. "You have a point there, John. That could be so. As you know, she's a wealthy woman now..."

"So?"

"Anita will be very careful about any man she chooses. A pastor is someone she can trust, the ideal person. How long do you believe she has been having thoughts about him?"

"Maybe a month or two before Alfred died. The death of Alfred has drawn her even closer to church. I truly don't know how closer she can get."

"She told me she needed more time," Peter said soberly.

"I don't think she sincerely means that, Peter. She did tell me that many times while deep down within she knew she was only trying to give me hope when there was none in reality."

"I hate being used, John!" Peter said angrily.

John saw a sudden change in his attitude. "I don't mean to hurt you, Peter, because you are a good man. I'm only warning you because I don't want you to get hurt like I did."

"Thanks, John. I appreciate that. I think you're right about Anita. Her heart is not with me. She only needs me to do my job there...nothing else!" Peter snapped.

"It's something to think about."

"Yet Leonora, I believe is very interested in me."

"I met her. Hmm, she is one raving beauty. That's a woman, Peter. What more could you want?"

"She isn't wealthy like Anita but she's beautiful. There's something about Anita, though...she's the type men can't resist. She's absolutely gorgeous."

"Yes, I fell into that trap. If Leonora likes you go for her then. The man that gets Anita is one lucky son of a..."

"Still angry! I can't blame you. I think I will have to start thinking hard in light of what you have told me," Peter said, a ring of confidence in his voice.

"Are you coming over?"

"No, I won't."

"What? Why?" a startled John asked.

"From now on, I'll only see her on business. Tell her I left this morning for Yardley Chase."

"To do what?" John asked, baffled by his decision not to go to see her.

"I'll go next week to see Leonora. Don't tell her that, though. Tell her I left town supposedly for Yardley Chase."

Meanwhile, Anita didn't know whether to feel disappointed or not, after John had informed her that Peter was out of town. She was inclined to believe that it might be better for her.

Pastor McIntosh came to the table where she had been sitting with Elizabeth, who left to go for a walk with John.

"No word from Peter?" Pastor McIntosh asked.

"John said he was out of town. His maid said he might have gone to Yardley Chase."

"Hmm, we're here and he's there."

"I'm certain if he knew we were coming he would have stayed," Anita mumbled.

"Who else we know here other than the local pastor?"

"No one."

"Then we have to try to make some friends."

"Dad had some old friends in the export business but I don't even remember their names."

"Your dad was well known in this town. He was also well respected."

"I would imagine that. He was a good man. I'm only sorry that our last years weren't spent better. I missed the hugs...the comforting words," Anita said, teary-eyed.

"I'm sorry. You deserve better than to agonize over it now," he said, placing his hand on her shoulder. It was the first time she recalled him doing that. No one else was around; she wondered if that spurred him to do that.

She stood up. A tear dropped out of her eye, then another crept down her face. Two more came after and then there was a steady flow that caused her body to jerk from the uncontrollable sobs. Anita wanted to cry to release some of her grief; the pastor's presence could have been a catalyst in this regard.

Pastor McIntosh came closer. Anita cried louder. He placed his arms around her. Anita flung her head on his shoulder. Where they were, it would have been difficult for anyone to see. They would have to know that they were already there. John and Elizabeth knew where they were. The other three pastors went for a walk. But Pastor McIntosh knew his actions could be viewed as inappropriate, should any of them bump into them. As a result, he didn't hold her for long. The nervous pastor gently lowered Anita back into the chair then sat around the table with her. She wiped her eyes clean; the image of his hand around her was already forming in her mind.

"Thank you so much," she said softly.

"For what?" Pastor McIntosh asked.

"For what you just did."

"That was nothing."

"What you did was much more than you think. You provide comfort. I've no one else to do that, Wilfred."

Footsteps came toward them. They came where they were; Elizabeth, John and the three pastors came into view.

"We found the church," Alton said.

"Yeah, is it far from here?" Anita asked.

"No, it's an easy walk. It's between those palm trees over there," he said, pointing at some trees.

"We can go now," Pastor McIntosh said.

The walk to Black River Baptist Church took fifteen minutes. On their way, they saw an Anglican church on the other side of the town. It was much bigger than the one they were going to. An elderly pastor welcomed them with open arms. Pastor Aaron Richards was very happy to see them. After the usual introductions, they got right down to the purpose of their visit.

The town of Black River was about to go to bed early. A few

lamp posts burning feebly along the main street were all that showed any sign of activity. There was no moon. The blackened sky was a glow of stars far and further away. The lamps could only shine a few feet; beyond that everything was drowned in darkness. All around, the insects were the rulers of the night. Fire flies and frogs were the dominant species.

Peter had been resisting the attempt all day to go to the inn where Anita and the rest were staying. He had been angry that this morning he made a hasty decision he had come to regret. Peter wanted to see Anita; he had to, or else he might go crazy. She would ask why he had gotten back so quickly. Peter planned to tell her he only went for a ride up to the Holland sugar plantation. He also did legal work for the owners there.

Peter had his supper, saddled his horse and rode to Logwood Inn. It was one straight road from where he lived; the horse had no problem finding its way in the dark.

After a day of discussions and meetings, the tired party from Yardley Chase joined the inhabitants of the town in their slumber, except for one person—Anita Campbell.

The snores from Elizabeth told her she was in dreamland. It was nearly ten o'clock. Even the innkeeper downstairs was fast asleep around his desk. But Anita couldn't sleep—that was far from her system.

Anita shoved her feet in the slippers by the bedside and walked through the door. She wished she could have bumped into Pastor McIntosh as soon as she went through the door. At least he would be someone to talk to until sleep invited her to come back in.

The sound of her slippers drawing against the floor woke the innkeeper. His head sprang from off the counter.

"Ohhh! I thought I heard something..." He yawned. Herbert Wilkinson was a small Scottish man with a tired-looking face. He owned the inn and his round-the-clock duties were enough reason for him to fall asleep around the check-in counter.

"I'm sorry to wake you. Had I known you were asleep, I would've just slipped by." Anita smiled.

"That's alright, ma'am."

"I couldn't sleep. I thought I would come down here for a while," Anita said, sitting in the chair beside the counter.

"That's alright, Miss Campbell. Your father stayed here on a few occasions. We talked right here on many nights like this. I find it amazing that you're doing the same thing." Herbert grinned.

"Oh! That's wonderful, like father, like daughter."

"I'm sorry to hear about his death. He was a very kind man."

"Most people I have met told me that. I guess they must be speaking the truth."

The sound of horses' hooves on the pavement outside caught their attention.

"You must have a late guest checking in," Anita mused.

"Ha! Ha! Ha! They check in all hours of the night, my dear."

The person walked to the counter, noticing the female presence nearby. It took him a few seconds to recognize Anita.

"Anita!"

"Peter!"

"What...I never expected to find you down here," Peter said, coming to face her. They embraced briefly.

"Hi, Peter. I fell asleep and she woke me. I was about to begin enjoying the conversation with her when you walked in," Herbert said, with no sign of drowsiness.

"Am I intruding on something here?"

"Come on, join the conversation. It's good," Anita said.

"I can see you two were having a good time. Where's the rest? My maid told me John came over shortly after I left."

"I thought you were out of town."

"I went up to Holland on business."

"Coffee for anyone? The pot is warm," Herbert interjected.

"I'm alright," Peter said.

"If I drink one, I won't sleep tonight. I couldn't sleep that's why I came down for a walk."

"We can go for one if you want," Peter said.

"Okay."

The twinkling stars were the only thing to greet them when they went out through the door.

"It's dark out here, where can we go?" Anita said.

"If it wasn't dark, I would have taken you on a tour of the area."

"That would have been nice. In this darkness, we can only walk out to the lamp post."

"Who's here with you?" Peter asked suddenly.

"Pastor McIntosh, three other pastors, John and Elizabeth, who also came with them from Kingston."

"Hmmm. You're in good company."

"Yes."

Peter wished he could have seen her expression in the dark but that was not possible. The light coming from the lamp post a few feet away didn't help one bit.

"You enjoy the company?"

"Of course I do. They are all friendly," Anita said as they walked closer to the light.

"Why did you come with them in the first place? I guess Yardley Chase must be getting boring," he asked, looking at her in the dark.

"Not really. Pastor McIntosh suggested I come along because it would do me some good."

"Oh. Was that the only reason for coming?"

Anita turned to look at him as they approached the lamp post. She could see his face much better. She suspected that Peter had a concern. "Well, yes and no. I knew I would see you. If he didn't invite me I wouldn't be here."

"If I had invited you, would you have come?"

"Maybe. So far, I can say that the outing has been good for me. It's truly a break from Yardley Chase. That place brings back many memories for me."

"Both good and bad."

"Yeah, both good and bad. Many times I asked God why so many undesirable things have been happening to me," Anita said, looking at the stars in the heavens.

"Did you get an answer?" Peter asked, looking up there, too.

"Not yet."

"One of the things I would want to know from God is whether the two of us will ever get married," Peter replied, still gazing at the stars above.

They came to the gate of the inn. Both of them leaned against the steel rails for support. A small gust of wind coming from the sea stirred the ginger lilies that were growing along the fence. It was not chilly but rather refreshing. It was one of those nights when you could walk and walk until your legs could carry you no more. Anita didn't want to go too far, in the event that Elizabeth woke up to find her missing. Anita hated to think what she would do: panic, scream for help or wake up the others who were getting a well-deserved rest.

"Have you been thinking about that a lot, Peter?" Anita asked, her thoughts drifting to Pastor McIntosh.

"I have to admit I do. Up to this morning, while I was talking to someone, I kept thinking about you wondering about that."

"What was the person talking about?"

"About a woman he suspected was in love with another man."

"Hmmm," Anita said, nodding her head. "Do you suspect me of that, too?"

"Are you?" Peter wanted to get that question out badly.

"Even if I did, I don't know if it would have been a smart thing to tell you...at least not right now."

"Why? That wouldn't be so trustworthy."

"If I'm one hundred percent sure I would tell you."

"Are you saying that there's someone you aren't certain about? I need to know, Anita..."

"I'm not certain at all but someone else is entering the picture and complicating matters...Leonora..." she said calmly.

"Ah I...let's assume that she's interested but the person doesn't have much choice."

"Then..." Anita said, not thinking about Peter and Leonora, rather Leonora and Pastor McIntosh.

"She's beautiful, you'll agree," Peter said, coming close enough to hold her hand in his. He wanted to do that.

"Okay, she is," Anita said abruptly, without giving the statement any thought.

"What would you do?"

"You're a man, you should answer that," she said.

Peter didn't find it humorous. A stern look possessed his face. "Go for the one you like best," he said, pausing for a while. "You're that one, Anita. As you're aware, having you isn't a certainty, though. Therefore, I must look at other possibilities."

"I couldn't blame you, Peter. You're a nice man who deserves a good wife. I need some more time. You wouldn't understand. If you have been through what I experienced over the years, you may have an idea why I'm in no rush."

"I've tried to picture myself in that position. It must have been hard for you I have to admit. Who feels it knows it. However, you may not like this, Anita, or I may sound a little harsh, but I firmly believe that there comes a time when one has to move on to forget the past."

"Easier said than done, Peter. You know that."

"Probably."

"Leonora is trying to get at me through whatever ways she can. I realize it's best to ignore her. I've been trying, but like I said I don't have much choice. I know she dislikes me. "

"How certain are you about that?"

"I've watched her movements and need no further conviction about that." Peter looked her in the dark, wishing he could comfort her in whatever ways she desired. "She's very lonely. And not many men are around. John...Pastor McIntosh."

Anita was caught off guard with the suggestion of that name. "Pastor McIntosh? Why would you think that?"

"She told me they talk a lot."

"A lot?"

"That's what she says. I don't see why she would be lying."

"Pastor McIntosh is there to minister to those in need. Who can tell, Leonora could have a spiritual matter that she needs some help with."

That was a smart answer, Anita, Peter said to himself. *You answered that one skillfully.* "Could it be that she needs no help at all and is only trying to make a little more than friendship?"

"That could jolly well be, Peter. She realizes that she's not making any headway, instead she's reaching out for you."

"Hmmm. I venture to say the safest thing to do isn't to make assumptions, rather to wait and see what will eventually happen."

"You're right on that one, Peter. I'm getting sleepy, we better go."

"You're right on that one, too, Anita."

They walked back to the inn. At the entrance, Peter reached out and kissed her lightly on the cheek, turned then walked to his horse.

Anita walked past the front desk. Herbert had his head down on the counter again. Anita didn't bother to disturb him. She continued to her room with some of Peter's questions echoing in her head. One thing she kept telling herself: Peter deserved better than how she was treating him.

The Black River Baptist Church had a good turnout for services on Sunday, morning. Most people hung around after service, talking and being introduced to the visiting pastors.

"You must have felt awkward with some people thinking you're my wife," Pastor McIntosh told Anita while they walked along the seashore later in the afternoon. Elizabeth, John and the others were walking ahead of them.

"Surprisingly I didn't. Let's say I tried to adjust myself to that situation," Anita laughed, almost aloud. In fact, she relished those brief minutes. She was happy and elated. At times, she corrected their mistakes, other times they moved on to another subject quickly, not giving either of them any time to explain anything.

"You really mean that? I thought you would be embarrassed."

"Embarrassed over what...for supposedly being your wife?"

"Er well, I don't mean it that way. I mean you aren't, and then, you're thinking you are. The embarrassing moment must be when you have to admit that you aren't."

"Even then, I wasn't ashamed. The times when I didn't have to explain made up for the time when you had to or I had to explain." Anita smiled convincingly.

"Anita, you're something else."

"I am." She laughed aloud again.

"I can see you are enjoying your time. I hope I'm right about that."

"You're right, I'm enjoying myself. It's nice out here. In Yardley Chase, you look at the sea every day. It's so far away from you. I'm walking right beside the sea here...I can reach down to touch the water," she said, doing exactly that as the remnant of a dying wave washed ashore, curling itself to return to the huge body of water.

"It's very nice here...quiet, relaxing. We...maybe I should come here more often."

"I would love to visit here more often. It's a breath of fresh air. When we get tired at looking at the sea we can get a boat to row up the river."

"You're sounding adventurous."

"A little of that is good sometimes. We don't know how longer we will be here. Why not enjoy life while we can."

"You can even enjoy it more when you have Jesus," Pastor McIntosh added.

"That's right. I've you to thank for that."

"It's a pity Peter is out of town. He would have been able to take us to some of the interesting places to see."

Guilt flowed into Anita's mind. She didn't want to reveal he had been to the inn last night. She trembled at any possible negative reaction from Wilfred. Somehow, she was convinced it was the right thing to do.

"I forget to mention that he came by last night," Anita said, nervously waiting for his reaction.

"Oh! When?"

"You were all asleep. I didn't want to wake you."

"Did he hang around for long?"

Anita was relieved he showed no sign of disappointment. She was too over cautious, Anita told herself. "As a matter of fact, he didn't stay long because he was returning from a short trip up north."

"Will we see him before we leave tomorrow?"

"I don't know because he didn't say. He sounded as if he was up to his waist in work."

"It's a pity maybe we won't see him."

"He's too busy for us." Anita smiled.

"We can make it up to him when next he comes to Yardley Chase."

"He might be busier then and not have the time for us."

Pastor McIntosh was at a loss regarding that statement.

CHAPTER 11

The trip to Black River was a memorable one for Anita. She thrived on that memory for several months; the visit was proving to have been a wise decision for many reasons. Pastor McIntosh got very busy right after the visit of the three pastors from Kingston. There were a few times when he had to go to the Flagaman church to preach to ensure everything was going well.

The usual chat after church services with Pastor McIntosh was almost a thing of the past for Anita. It was something she couldn't understand. She understood his tiredness and preoccupation with church duties. Somehow, what she failed to comprehend was the provoking scene Anita had to confront each Sunday with Leonora. She took over nearly all the duties at church, from serving refreshments to organizing the choir. As a result of her duties, she used every available opportunity to consult Pastor McIntosh, apparently on trivial matters.

All Anita could do these days was to recollect the Black River and Kingston trips. She became disgusted at being totally ignored that she was tempted to stop going to church. One night while she was praying, she realized that one of the main reasons for going to church was to get closer to God, not the pastor. The bottom line was God was the one responsible for helping her pull through tough times.

Peter came to Yardley Chase once since the Black River trip, the only one she could confirm. She got a shock one Monday morning when she saw Peter galloping through the gate. Anita thought he was coming for a visit, although it seemed somewhat strange that he was coming on Monday morning. Peter stopped briefly to say hello. He informed Lynda he had spent the weekend at the Simmonds', and was on his way back home.

Immediately, Lynda knew something was wrong. Later in the day, Anita told her what had happened in Black River. Surprisingly, Lynda didn't look disappointed; she told her daughter to be very careful because she was now a rich woman, thus someone could want to marry quickly for the wrong reason. Lynda had no reservations about Peter in that regard, although she couldn't be one hundred percent positive.

John made two trips to Kingston. On the last one, a month ago, he returned to break the news that he and Elizabeth were getting married in December. Anita was very happy for him. She could see how much he had been looking forward to that.

John also informed Anita of Andrew's progress in Kingston. To her dismay, Andrew had become active in politics, even taking part in some demonstrations in Kingston. On one occasion, he had visited an area of St. Thomas where a local Baptist preacher had been organizing demonstrations against the deplorable conditions facing former slaves. That was what Andrew wanted to do. Anita was glad his dreams were coming true.

Anita could tell her mother wasn't over her grieving for her father. John was busy in his own little world. Andrew was away, and of course Pastor McIntosh was either busy or wasn't up to talking to her. Undoubtedly, Anita felt ostracized and slipped into a very stressful period.

Lynda drifted further away from her, especially since Peter's revelation that he had stayed with the Simmonds one weekend. Lynda slept a lot, and the smell of alcohol gradually took over her room. While Lynda found solace in whiskey, Anita found it at Lover's Leap—the exact spot her lover jumped to death with another slave. Every day, shortly after breakfast,

Anita rode out to the cliff and stayed there for several hours, looking out into the blue sky and sea and the vegetation below. She remembered the nights she had spent there. Even though it happened long ago, the images were vivid and defined.

Sally bumped into her one morning while she was having a sun bath. Sally hadn't gone there in a while and decided to go there for relaxation. There was nothing much to do except to relax in the warmth of the sun with the cool wind blowing all over you.

"Hi, Miss Anita?" Sally said softly, trying not to frighten her because Anita didn't see her coming.

"Huh, Oh! Sally! What are you...you almost frightened me," she said, turning around to face her.

"Sorry, ma'am, but I couldn't help it." Sally came up to sit beside her on the rock where Anita was resting.

"It's alright, Sally, I'm not dying of fright," Anita said with a smile. "How are you doing? How's Simon and Jerry? I haven't seen them for a while."

"Alright, ma'am. Dem working wid Mas' John."

"You're not working?"

"No, ma'am. Sometimes I get some work at di church."

"Oh! With Pastor McIntosh."

"Yes, ma'am, but I..."

"Is there a problem?" Anita asked quickly because the subject had to do with Pastor McIntosh.

"Ah, I did somet'ing...I don't know if a should say it, ma'am," Sally said, looking away from her.

"You don't have to say if you don't want to do that," Anita said, hoping she would eventually blurt it out.

"Y'know, maybe it's not serious."

"Why worry?"

"It's jus' dat I don't feel comfortable dere, ma'am."

"Why? You should be comfortable because he's a nice person."

"True, ma'am. It's not Pastor McIntosh, ma'am," Sally said, opening up her thoughts a bit.

"Well, who..."

"Dat lady, ma'am, di woman who dress up nice every

Sunday, ma'am," Sally said, giving into Anita's line of questioning.

"You mean...Ah what's her name...ah Leonora."

"Yes, ma'am. Dat is di one."

"What about her, Sally?"

"She...she asked mi fi duh somet'ing fi har, ma'am. A don't feel comfortable doing it, ma'am."

"Doing what?"

"Hmmm, she want mi fi tell her who come to di house to see Pastor."

Anita was puzzled. "Why would she do that?" she asked curiously.

"She did not tell mi, ma'am. I t'ink she jus' want to know if him seeing anyone."

"But Pastor McIntosh sees a lot of people as he's always helping them with their problems."

"Dat's true, ma'am. She mus' be jealous," Sally said mockingly.

"Jealous, she has no reason to be jealous. Pastor McIntosh is more interested in his work more than anything else."

Sally paused for a while, glancing at the roaring waves below. "A t'ink she's jealous a yuh, ma'am."

Anita's blood ran cold. The initial shock gave her an instant headache. She felt frozen in time and thought. Words bombarded her thought process as she tried to formulate a sentence that wouldn't make Sally any wiser. "What are you talking...talking about, Sally? Jealous of what?"

"Maybe she t'ink yuh gettin' too much attention from Pastor...Hmmm, I t'ink Pastor likes you, too," Sally said, her gaze still fixed on the frothy pattern of the waves forming below.

Anita searched for the right answer again. "Pastor likes everybody," she said, trying to project lucidity in her voice.

"The whole a Yardley Chase know dat him like yuh, Miss Anita," Sally said innocently.

"What? Where did you get all this nonsense?" Anita emerged from her seat in a rage. She calmed down quickly. "Sorry for sounding harsh but where did you get that from, Sally?" Anita asked, hands akimbo.

"I hear people talkin' a church, ma'am," she said. Anita's reaction had frightened her. She tried to avoid her eyes.

"Have mercy! Do you mean that? Are you sure? How long has this been going on, Sally?"

"After yuh come back from Kingston, ma'am."

There was a minute of silence. "What am I going to do? I didn't know all that was happening?"

"Yuh 'fraid of what people sayin', ma'am?"

"Yes. It could harm the church and Pastor as well."

"True, Miss Anita. What yuh goin' to do?"

"The only thing I can think of is to stay away for a while. Sally, I'm going to ask you not to discuss this with anyone; do you understand? Come over to my house a few days per week. I'll find some work for you, okay."

"Okay, ma'am."

All afternoon, Anita had a severe headache. The only thing on her mind now was Leonora. Who else could be responsible for that gossip? She had good reason to spread rumour. Leonora, it seemed, had every intention of gaining Pastor McIntosh and Peter's attention—at all costs.

On Sunday morning, Anita slept very late being the first in a long time that she wouldn't be going to church. Lynda didn't see her come for breakfast and took a cup of tea up to her bedroom. Anita appeared to be sleeping when she walked in; she turned at the sound of the footsteps easing herself up into a sitting position.

"Are you alright? Aren't you going to church?"

"I'm so tired, Mom, that I feel like I could sleep the entire day."

"Here," Lynda said, handing her the cup and saucer. "We all need a break—a real break."

"You definitely need a break, Mom. Take some time off to go somewhere, maybe to England."

"England? No, I couldn't take that journey, dear," she remarked, sitting at the side of the bed.

"How about Kingston?"

Lynda rubbed her eyes. "Y'know, come to think of it maybe I should. I haven't been there for a while. I should have gone with you when Andrew left. Do you want to come?"

"We both can't leave here, Mom."

"Good old John is here. There's no better."

Such a trip could get her away from the drinking. Anita knew she couldn't turn him down. Furthermore, Anita could barely wait to see Andrew.

"We could take Simon and Jerry. They would be glad to see Andrew."

"I know," Lynda said, nodding. "They need something to do, too. We can leave tomorrow if that's okay with you."

"I wish I could leave right now." Anita grinned.

"I'll ride over there to tell them right now."

"Thanks, Mom. You made my day."

Anita was glad to be getting away from Yardley Chase. She would miss two more Sundays without going to church. On top of that, she had a good excuse not to attend. The thought of informing Pastor McIntosh about her pending departure came to mind. Anita thought about it for a while, ultimately dismissing the idea. She kept herself busy throughout the day by starting to pack her traveling bag. Sally came over to give a hand; Anita briefed her about what she could do while she was away.

Pastor McIntosh tried to remember if he had seen Anita at church last Sunday. He had been awfully busy making arrangements for John's wedding that he didn't have much time on Sunday for anyone. Leonora had been of great help, and he didn't know what he would have done without her.

Anita had also missed the Wednesday night prayer meeting; Pastor McIntosh was convinced something was wrong. He had to admit he hadn't been talking much to Anita these days. He had always looked forward to talking before and after service. It hadn't been that way in a long time. Why? The pastor searched for answers, only to come up with no clear explanation. All he could remember was that, in recent weeks, he had been trying to assist Leonora in organizing the choir. Dr. Simmonds, who had been attending every week, was always at choir practice, mainly observing. They got into long conversations on a few occasions. By the time that was all over, Anita had disappeared.

Pastor McIntosh sat around his desk pondering the recent after-service events. How could he fail to ignore Anita that much? From all indications, she didn't get over the sudden death of her father. She needed someone to talk to on a regular basis.

The first chore on Pastor McIntosh's list of duties was to pay Anita a visit. John was feeding the chickens when he saw him coming.

"Hey, Pastor, come right over. How's the morning, sir?"

"It's a good morning, John. Let us give thanks for that," he said, patting him on the shoulder.

"Getting nervous for that wedding?"

"To be honest with you, yes, sir, I am. I keep asking myself how I am going to get over this significant milestone in my life."

"You will, don't worry about that."

"Andrew must be missing old Teddy here," he said, pointing at the rooster.

"If Anita could have carried her, on Monday, I think she would have done that." John grinned.

"You mean she went to Kingston?" Wilfred asked unexpectedly.

"You didn't know? I thought she had told you. She, Lynda, Jerry and Simon left on Monday."

"How long will they be there for?"

"Lynda says she needs a long rest. Whatever that means, sir, they could end up being there for a while."

"Huh, they need a break."

"They sure do, sir. They've been through a lot."

"I guess you're running the operations here. You're a good man, John. Alfred trusted you all these years and Lynda is doing the same. That's commendable."

"Thank you, sir. Those are very kind words."

"You deserve them, John. Elizabeth is getting a nice husband."

"Ha! Ha! Ha! You're making me blush. An old man like me will find it hard to adjust to this new life," John said, putting down a pan containing the corn.

Both men stooped to the ground, apparently ready for an early morning conversation.

"We're never too old to learn. You aren't old, John."

"Me, sir, huh, I should've been married long ago."

"I'm curious, why didn't you?" Pastor McIntosh asked, using a piece of stick to draw lines in the loose dirt where he was stooping.

"The woman I wanted to marry didn't want me." He shrugged.

"You've taken it in good humor, John," Pastor McIntosh said, his eyes moving from the ground up into his face.

"Only now, sir, years ago I was a broken-hearted man. I loved this woman to death; sometimes I think I still do, but she totally rejected me. The worst thing for me is to see her practically every day."

"Anita!"

"Yes. Anita has been the love of my life," John said calmly.

"Who wouldn't fall in love with her? She's a beautiful woman." He smiled.

John was tempted to ask him if he was in love with her. Because of the respect he had for the pastor, being a spiritual leader, John refrained from asking that question. "The situation has turned around. Anita introduced me to Elizabeth in Kingston. I believe that was where it all started," John said confidently, an element of pride and triumph in his voice.

"Anita wants to see you happy. She knows of your disappointment in her and wants to make it up. She's kind-hearted like her father."

"That's true, sir. Sometimes I wish she would find a nice husband," John remarked, avoiding his eyes.

"She will in time. Anita is a rich woman. She has it all and who could resist that?"

"She can pick, choose, refuse whoever she wants. If that slave was alive, she would have no problem."

"Anita loved him that much?"

"I've never seen a woman love a man the way she did," John said sincerely. "After a time, I knew my chances with her were almost zero. Although I refused to accept that, I can see how wrong I was in thinking I had a chance. If she should ever love someone like that again, he'll be a lucky man."

"Hmmm, you should know, John. You've been here with her all these years."

"I'm waiting with abated breath to see who'll go down the aisle with her."

"I hope I'll be a part of that wedding ceremony." Pastor McIntosh smiled.

"You'll be the first to know," John said teasingly.

Anita, Lynda, Jerry and Simon rolled into Kingston, on Friday. The afternoon was hot, the humidity intense, the dusty streets a strain on the eyes. They were happy to be shielded in the confines of the Baptist Mission. Andrew was sitting in the lunchroom when they walked in. He sprang from his seat at the sight of his mother and grandmother.

"My goodness! My goodness! What are you doing here?" He ran straight into his mother's arms, reaching out to Lynda in the process. "Boy, am I glad to see you all...Jerry, Simon."

"It's good to see you, too, Andrew. My goodness! Look at you...you look really well," Anita said, releasing his grip to examine him from head to toe.

"Grandma! You look wonderful!" Andrew embraced her like he was a lost child that had been found.

"Kingston is having a good effect on you, too, Andrew."

"It's alright, I cannot complain. Jerry! Simon! How are you doing?" Andrew said, turning to both of them.

"We're alright, sah! Glad to see yuh, sah," Jerry said.

"Have you eaten?" Andrew asked.

"We could do with some food," Simon suggested.

Anita recognized Robert Barnes walking over to them. He was the gentleman whom they met when they came there first.

"It's good to see you again, Miss Campbell," he said with outstretched arms.

"Hello, Mr. Barnes, how are you?" Anita said. "Meet my mom, Lynda, and Jerry and Simon."

"Hello, everybody. It's good to see you all. You must be

hungry. We'll get you some food and we can talk after," Mr. Barnes said, heading for the kitchen.

Andrew walked with Anita outside after the meal, while Lynda and Robert remained inside talking. Jerry and Simon had disappeared somewhere.

"Is everything alright, Mom? I'm surprised to see you."

"Everything is fine, Andrew. We never planned it. Mom, who you know has been going under a lot of pressure since Dad's death, deserves a vacation or break. We decided to come here instead."

"I can't get over Grandfather. It doesn't look real. I keep reading your letter over and over again. The break is good for you. They have lodgings here for a small fee, much more than you need."

"We don't know how long we'll be staying, all we need is a break from Yardley Chase. John will take care while we are away."

"We can rely on John. Elizabeth is here, excited about the wedding," Andrew laughed. "She'll be glad to see you to fill her in on what has been happening down there with John."

"How's life here, Andrew?" Anita asked as both of them sat down under a tree.

"It's going great, Mom. I cannot complain. I've been going to meetings and even attended a few marches. I've learned a lot, Mom. There are some very dedicated men in Kingston, who want better living and working conditions for former slaves. I wish my father could see me at work."

"I'm glad to hear that, Andrew," Anita replied, the mention of Jerome stirring her interest. "I truly wish he were here, too..."

"The authorities have been on guard to ensure there's no violence at these meetings. I understand the Governor is keeping a close watch on everything," he said cautiously.

"Be careful, Andrew."

"No, I'm alright, Mom. You don't have to worry about me. My mission is to sit in the House of Assembly to represent the oppressed of this country who're former slaves."

"Jerome would be proud of you, Andrew," Anita said, rubbing her hand over his arms. "I miss him terribly, Andrew. I miss you, too."

"Please understand that even in death, I want to do this for him, Mom. I have to get involved in the active part of politics because one day I want to represent the voters."

"I understand, son. I've been making that sacrifice to have you here. How long will that take?"

"Years. Some things have started to happen in St. Thomas. I may take a trip out there some time soon."

"Who'll take you?" she asked, concern in her voice.

"I already know some local politicians. Some church leaders are more than willing to take me. This movement needs men, Mom—strong men to lead, to come up with practical ideas, draft policies, organize meetings to get the goals of our mission out to the poor people. I'm convinced I can play a part in this, Mom."

"You're already sounding like a politician, Andrew," Anita said mockingly.

"At least someone is recognizing that," Andrew grinned sheepishly.

Leonora Simmonds didn't expect Peter Bradley to show up on her steps tonight—at least not for now. Regardless of what she might have thought, Peter was there on Friday night, having come for another weekend. Leonora's home was where he stayed on the last two visits.

"Look who's here," Leonora blurted out, her father coming up behind her.

"Who's there?" Dr. Simmonds asked.

"It's Peter."

"Hi, hello. I hope I'm not imposing too much."

"Please don't say it that way. You're welcome to stay here anytime," Dr. Simmonds said.

"We were about to have supper...you're right on time."

Peter enjoyed the supper partly because he was hungry. After supper, they talked for a while before Dr. Simmonds retired for bed.

Leonora didn't wait for long to let Peter know what she had been thinking.

"I don't think Pastor McIntosh would be pleased knowing you're staying here, Peter. For me, it's okay; for him, I doubt if that would go down well with him."

Peter was shocked out of his wits. Where did this idea come from so suddenly?

"I don't understand. How does he come into this picture, may I ask?"

"Well, over the past few weeks, I've taken a leading role in the affairs of the church. I think you could say I have to live a respectable life."

"When you say leading role, what do you mean?" Peter asked, evidently puzzled.

"I'm organizing, or re-organizing the choir, doing treasury duties, among other things."

"Hmmm. Nothing else?"

"No. I think that's enough."

Peter recognized that this Leonora was a different one from the one he had last seen.

"I guess this is going to be my last night here," Peter managed to say.

"I'm sorry, Peter, I didn't mean to disappoint you in any way."

"I can hardly believe this is the Leonora I met earlier this year. You were all excited to see me, and were even contemplating going down to Black River with me for a week. Tonight, you don't want to see me. What has gotten over you, Leonora?"

Leonora meditated on his assertions for a few seconds before answering. "Let's say I'm trying to live a life right in the sight of God."

"What are we doing that is wrong? We're not sharing the same bed."

"I know. The point is it doesn't look good from the outside."

"Does anyone, apart from the pastor, know I'm staying here?" Peter inquired.

"Yardley Chase is a small community. I guarantee they'll know you'll be sleeping here for a second time tonight."

"Did they know about the first?" Peter asked, clasping his hand in front of his face.

"They did. That's why I have to be taking precautions now."

"Does your father know what's going on?"

"No, I'm trying to stop it before he hears anything."

"Tell me the truth, Leonora, do you have anything going with that pastor?" he asked abruptly.

Leonora rose from her chair, her fingers fumbling over each other. "What a question? Why would you ever think of such a question? He's a man of God, called by God to do his work, to minister to His people. Where would he find time for me? Why would he want me anyway when there's the beautiful and rich Anita Campbell, heiress to the throne at Jack's Place?"

"I see, that's it," Peter said, nodding his head in agreement to whatever he was thinking.

"That's what, Peter?"

"This is a competition business. It's all about competition with Anita. You're trying to outdo each other in order to win attention from the pastor who doesn't even have a clue on what's going on."

"Hmmm, why not? He's the only eligible bachelor within miles around," Leonora said, facing Peter.

"You're admitting that this is what it's all about?" Peter asked, sounding triumphant this time around.

"You're the one saying that," Leonora replied, not wishing to add anything more to that comment.

"Are you aware that Anita is far ahead of you?"

"In terms of what?"

"Well, they've been to Kingston together, Black River once, and he visits her quite often," Peter said rather vindictively.

The light from the lamp shining feebly across the room didn't hide Leonora's reddened face.

"I know that. You may be disappointed to know that all that has changed in recent weeks. Anita hasn't been to church recently; neither has Pastor McIntosh been over there to see her."

"How do you know that?"

"I have my ways of knowing," Leonora said, remembering

Sally's last words to her. According to Sally, she was certain Pastor hadn't been visiting Anita. Sally believed that something had gone wrong with their relationship. Leonora was delighted to hear that, although she was displeased with Sally's lack of enthusiasm in informing her.

"Are you saying that Anita is no longer interested in him?"

"How did you know in the first instance that she was interested?"

"Let's say I have my way of knowing, too," he said, hitting back at her.

"Oh! We're into competition here."

"On all fronts. To think of it, I'm realizing that the competition is getting too hot for me. I have to pull out," Peter said, throwing up his hands into the air.

"You shouldn't give up. Have you truly given up on Anita?"

"I've already done that. When I leave here tomorrow morning, I'll be giving up on you, too," Peter said, raising his voice a little.

"You're leaving tomorrow? I thought you were going to stay the whole weekend."

"I cannot stay where I'm not welcomed. If it was daylight, I would be in the saddle already heading for home."

"I'm sorry, Peter. I'm truly sorry it had to end like this," Leonora moaned pitifully.

"It never started. Be sorry for yourself, Leonora. I hate to tell you this, but don't be surprised if one day you end up getting hurt."

"Don't worry your handsome head, I won't," Leonora said, rubbing her hand in Peter's head.

Anita and Lynda had been getting a taste of city life all week. From dinner parties to political meetings, they had a fairly good idea of how interesting life could be in the capital. No wonder Andrew was enjoying himself—such a contrast to life in Yardley Chase.

Elizabeth had been of great help. She was only too happy to take them around places of interest to let them feel at home. Andrew spent a lot of time with Jerry and Simon. They accompanied him to political meetings on two occasions. Anita had a better understanding of the reasons for Andrew's decision to go into politics. The tone of the meetings all had one thing in common: to serve the people in building a new society, especially the underprivileged and the working poor. A new breed of young politicians, several mulattos among them, was becoming a very vocal group in the House of Assembly. Andrew had found common ground with which to pursue his political ambitions in this make-up of newcomers.

Anita and Lynda had been unaware of the days flashing by. Constant engagement in one form of activity or another had kept them quite busy. At the end of two weeks, Anita caught up on the number of days they had been in Kingston. She was astonished that during that time Pastor McIntosh and the challenges at Yardley Chase didn't come to mind. Jerome did, though. As hard as it was to admit it, their memorable times together provided comfort each night before she fell asleep. The recollections didn't hurt that much; somehow they comforted her.

"Are you getting homesick?" Andrew asked his mother shortly after Sunday services.

"I don't even know," Anita said, enjoying a cool afternoon under one of the two weeping willow trees on the church compound. "The moment I return to Yardley Chase, I'll be right back to where I started," she said jokingly.

"I was homesick for some time. I do get homesick at times."

"I've never been away from home this long. I'm surprised I've lasted this long without getting those feelings."

"Is everything alright with you back in Yardley Chase, Mom?" That question had been tickling Andrew's brain for a while.

"What do you mean, son?" She saw a look of concern in Andrew's eyes; she wanted to satisfy his curiosity as much as possible.

"I know because Dad isn't around anymore, your life is in the church. I know you want to settle down in order to move on with your life. And that's fine with me, Mom. Has there been any progress with that?"

"Hmmm, I'm listening to the words of a mature son. I'm proud of you, Andrew; you've truly grown up. It's true I've been thinking about that. I'd like you to know I'm not in any rush. When the right one comes along, we'll see where it goes from there." She smiled.

"John is a lucky man. I'm happy for him. Elizabeth talks about him almost every day."

"She'll be happy. John will make a good husband. It's a role he has been waiting to play for many years. I guess his time has come. Similarly, my time will come soon."

"I can see you are a woman of faith."

"Pastor McIntosh has taught me well." She smiled.

"I know he means a lot to you spiritually..." Andrew said, turning his head away from his mother.

"I couldn't deny that. He's a wonderful man who has taught me the Word of God, how meaningful life can be if you live for Jesus."

"I'll always remember him for his kindness to me, for helping you. Because my father isn't alive, I see him as some sort of role model for me. It's a pity he wasn't around in my younger days."

"It's good to hear you say that about him, Andrew. You should write him a letter telling him how you feel."

Andrew rubbed the few strands of hair peeping out from under his chin. "I should've done that long ago. You know what, Mom, I'm going to give you a letter to take to him," he said, elated that his mother had made the suggestion at the right time.

"That would be great, Andrew."

"Have you decided when you'll leave? I notice Grandma doesn't seem to be in any hurry."

"I'm in no hurry either, Andrew. Anytime she wishes to go I'm ready."

"You mean you haven't missed church, especially the wonderful sermons by Pastor McIntosh?"

"I cannot deny that I miss church. You don't really know how much you miss it until you're away from it. I'll survive, though; there's a saying that goes 'absence makes the heart grows fonder.' I know when I return I'll appreciate it much more."

"Pastor McIntosh's sermons will be like an oasis. I'm certain he'll be glad to see you," Andrew chirped.

Anita smiled not knowing what, if anything, to make of that statement.

"I've seen you before," Peter Bradley told the young girl standing before him.

"I saw yuh with Miss Leonora," Sally said.

"Oh! Oh! You're right," Peter said, standing on the steps of the entrance to Lynda's house. Sally, who was coming through the door, almost bumped into Peter.

"I was on my way to Black River…thought I would stop to say hello to Mrs. Campbell," Peter said.

"Oh! Mrs. Campbell an' her dawta is not here, sah," she said boldly.

"When will they be back?"

"Oh! Yuh don't understan', sah, dem is away—far away," Sally said, indicating by hand that they weren't anywhere near there.

"England?"

"No, no, no, not England, sah, in Kingston."

"Oh! Kingston. I see, is John here, or he went with them?"

"John is working over there, sah," Sally said, pointing in the direction of the cane fields.

"Thank you er…"

"Sally, sah. I work fo' Miss Anita."

"You work for Anita?"

"Yes, sah, very hard, too, sah. She treat mi good, sah, not like di others."

"Who else do you work for, Sally?" Peter asked, wondering where the dialogue was leading him.

"I work fo' Miss Leonora, too, sah."

"What kind of work do you do for her?"

"All kinds of work. I do everyt'ing for her, sah, to mek sure they go alright. It's hard work, sah."

"I'm sure it's hard work. She's a busy woman, especially at church."

"Oh! Yes, sah. She worked hard at church helpin' Pastor. Di church people even talk 'bout it a lot, sah."

"Hmm, that's interesting." Peter grinned under his breath. That was it; Sally was the one bringing word to Leonora about the gossiping. He got his answers.

Peter found John daydreaming, while the laborers in the field toiled to earn their daily wages.

He sat leaning against a tree in the cool of the shade with his eyes staring out at the powdery-white clouds mingled with patches of the blue sky.

"You must be thinking of something nice," Peter said calmly.

John's head jerked in Peter's direction. A grin rippled across his fleshy face the moment he recognized Peter.

"Come right over here, m'boy...enjoy some of life's more rewarding pleasures," John said proudly.

"I can see you're on top of this world."

"The world was on top of me for many years, Peter. It's the reverse today. I'm getting married to Elizabeth, Peter. Believe me, it's going to be the happiest time of my life."

Peter raised his eyebrows, obviously pleased with what he was hearing. "I'm very happy for you, John. I know it's a good feeling."

"Words aren't enough to explain it. Imagine me getting married. The wedding is only weeks away...hmm, sometimes I cannot even accept it," John said, rubbing his jaw.

"You'll in time, don't you worry about that."

"I have to be grateful to Anita. If it wasn't for her, I'd be here languishing in my loneliness."

"Are you telling me she had a role in this?" Peter asked, sitting down on the grass beside John.

"She introduced me to Elizabeth when we were in Kingston. That was where it all started," John said, almost boastfully.

"Hmmm, the same woman whom you have been crazy about

is responsible for providing a wife for you—another woman. That's rather cute."

"Ah! Peter, life is a mystery. It's difficult to understand a woman."

"They could say the same about us," Peter laughed.

"I can only leave a woman like Anita to you, Peter. I'm only a poor overseer, while your status is much higher than mine. You would be good for her," John advised him.

"That's history, John. I haven't seen Anita in a long time. I hope to keep it that way. Why should I bother wasting my time with her?"

"Why are you here?"

"I stopped by to see Lynda to deal with some legal matters."

"Oh! Well, as you can see, they're off on vacation. The pastor isn't with them, only two laborers from here. She stayed away from church for a while before she went to Kingston. Do you get the message?" John inquired, emphasizing the question to send home a message.

"Something may be wrong?"

"Exactly."

Peter looked at the laborers chopping away at the cane plants, the sweat-soaked clothes sticking onto their skin. The sun was showering out all its energy on them. He couldn't stay in that sweltering heat for a minute. *Poor souls*, he thought.

"My patience ran out on Anita. I don't want to get hurt, it's best I let her be."

"You honestly mean that, or that new lady, the talk of Yardley Chase, has been catching your eyes?" John stared at him, being quite conscious of the fact that he would soon be a married man, and wouldn't have to worry about getting a woman.

"That's not working out either, John. I think I have some more waiting to do," Peter said, pulling up some weeds while he spoke.

"Look, I've waited for nearly thirty years. Here I am only weeks away. It was painful sometimes. I have to admit that; however, I don't think it will be like that anymore. I know I've found a good woman."

"I truly wish you the best, John. I mean it from the bottom of my heart."

"Thanks, Peter, I know you mean it. I want to wish you well, too, hoping you'll soon find someone. "

"I will. Believe me I will," Peter said confidently.

CHAPTER 12

Yardley Chase had been a beehive of talk over the past few weeks. The talk was about John's planned marriage to Elizabeth. No wedding had taken place in the district in the past two years. Naturally, the next one would be the center of attraction.

John was known throughout Yardley Chase. He knew that if he invited a few members of the community, the whole district would be there. Hence, the invitation was open to everyone. John had planned to slaughter a whole cow, three goats, and several chickens. He had been living in the tropics too long not to realize that occasions like a wedding had started to take on the image of a great feast.

Lynda offered Jack's Place to be the venue for the occasion. All her staff was assigned to help with the preparations.

It was Sunday morning. The wedding would be on the following Saturday. Sundays had become a long and boring day for Anita. Since she returned from Kingston five weeks ago, she had only been to church once. Leonora's masquerade had been intensifying in recent weeks. She was as busy as a bee. The results were obvious, as Anita had to admit the church looked pretty organized.

Pastor McIntosh had left right after service for another trip to Flagaman. Anita barely managed to get a hello from him a few minutes before service started. Leonora ensured that there was no dialogue between them. She butted right in to inform the pastor there was something she wanted to discuss with him.

On this rather cool Sunday morning, the prospect of another of Leonora's mocking displays of triumph made Anita shudder. She couldn't stand another day of it. Whatever Leonora had up her sleeve she would get it without her presence.

"Aren't you going to church?" Lynda asked, walking up to Anita. She had been sitting beside the well—her favorite spot to meditate and reflect on the good times with Jerome. In times of duress, Anita would go to that spot, something she had been doing even before she met Jerome.

"I don't get the drive to go anymore," she said dryly.

"What? I don't believe you, not the Anita who was so wrapped up in church up to last month," a wide-eyed Lynda said, staring at her. "Is something wrong?"

"It's a long story, Mom."

"I'd surely like to know why. I've all the time in the world," Lynda said, sitting down beside her.

Anita knew her mother that long to conclude that she wanted to help. "Church is fine, my belief in God is as strong as ever. The problem is with the people."

"People? You mean Pastor McIntosh?"

"No, to be more specific, one person."

"Leonora."

"How did you know that?" she asked quickly.

"Instinct. The first day I met her I could tell she's a domineering woman, who'll do anything to get what she wants."

"And what does she want?"

"Pastor McIntosh."

Anita tried to hide her amazement. Lynda knew what had been going on at church. It was an indication that someone could be feeding her information on what had been happening.

"Mom, whatever made you think of that? Pastor McIntosh isn't looking for a wife. He's too busy with his church."

"That's precisely why Leonora is behaving like that. She's trying to get his attention and she doesn't want anyone to come into her way," Lynda said, holding on to her arm.

"She's doing a good job of that."

"Leonora suspects you like Pastor, hence her motive in sidelining and undermining you. Have you been talking a lot with Pastor?"

"Nope, he has been spending a lot less time with me the last few times I went to church."

"Ah! You see what I'm saying. I wish I could get the opportunity to tell her she's fighting a losing battle."

"How do you know she's losing?"

"Because Pastor McIntosh isn't interested in her. If, and I emphasize if, he's interested in any woman at this stage, it's you," Lynda said, smiling.

"What makes you think so?" Anita asked, appreciative of that suggestion.

"The way he looks at you carries enough evidence that he admires you a lot. The problem, I suspect, is shyness. It may be hard to believe because he's up on the pulpit, however, it may be awkward for him to express his true feelings for you. To make matters worse, you're a rich woman."

"You like him, Mom?"

"I must admit I was hoping you and Peter would've got together. After a while, I could see that it wasn't working out."

"He wants me to marry him. I told him I need some more time," Anita said softly, images of a smiling Jerome slipping through unexpectedly.

"That's because you're only thinking about Pastor."

A tear sprang from out of its gland, a sob burst through Anita's lips, and within seconds, there were many others emerging from their hidden domain. *My dear Jerome*, she thought. How was she ever going to get over him? Anita's hands reached out like a crab's claws and grabbed her mother's shoulder. Her head found her chest, and rested on it like a young babe seeking maternal comfort to soothe its cries.

A mother's maternal instinct reached out to familiar territory, welcoming the presence of a long weaned offspring. Age didn't make a difference here, because the memories of yesteryear began to flood the mind that nurtured and cared for this fruit of its womb, until it was ready to survive with parental guidance.

The moment was one of emotional exchanges; the reunification of decades' old bonds also triggered tears from the other end. The result: tears of joy, tears of sorrow. The realization that what was good for daughter would bring happiness to mother, was more than enough to warrant a tighter embrace.

Anita sobbed uncontrollably on her mother's bosom. Lynda allowed Anita to pour out all her tears on her. The tears seeped through her thin dress, making Lynda feel the wetness against her chest. In a sense, it felt good, really good. Those were the tears of her grown up "baby," that Lynda didn't have the opportunity of holding and comforting in a long, long time. Some of Anita's tears were still for Jerome, but he was far from Lynda's mind.

"I know how you feel, my dear, you don't have to say it. I'm certain he's thinking that way, too. It's only a matter of time before the two of you will have to face the fact that you cannot hide from each other anymore."

Pastor McIntosh had delivered another powerful sermon, exhorting the brethren never to give up on God in the face of trying circumstances. Tired as he was, McIntosh did a splendid job of reinforcing the need to live in the hope that Jesus had gone to prepare a better place for His people.

After service, Leonora invited him to dinner, an invitation he gladly accepted. As he had been discovering recently, Leonora was a good cook. He was too tired to cook for himself, making any such invitation a timely treat.

Pastor McIntosh saw two riders coming toward him on his way from dinner. The riders were two people he hadn't seen in quite a while—Lynda and Anita. He re-arranged his thoughts to note the fact that Anita hadn't been to church for a while. Neither had he visited Jack's Place since the last time Lynda and Anita went to Kingston. Was he missing out on something?

"Whoa...hold it right there," Pastor McIntosh said, almost

blocking the pathway of the two oncoming riders. "How are you all doing?"

"We're surviving...getting along as you can see," Lynda answered.

"That I can see, it's also a nice afternoon for a ride," he suggested.

"That we are doing. How are you doing?" Lynda asked.

"Lots of work...I'm too busy to notice that." He grinned.

"You're a busy man, we won't keep you...you take care of yourself," Lynda said, with the horses moving off in the intended directions.

"Remember, don't give up on church," Pastor McIntosh said, speaking above the sound of the galloping horses.

"We won't, "Lynda shouted back.

All the way home, Pastor McIntosh's bewildered mind agonized over Anita's failure to exchange at least one word with him during their brief encounter. She looked at him with an expression that made it difficult to decipher whether she was smiling or not. Strangely, that was unlike the Anita he thought he knew. Something was wrong. He entered his house thinking that way, and when he jumped into his bed, that belief was firmly affixed in his mind.

Pastor McIntosh found sleep drifting away from him instead of drawing closer. The thought of Anita sitting in the saddle beside her mom, not saying a word to him, had been haunting his thoughts ever since. He tried to remember what had happened on the last two occasions she came to church. There was nothing out of the ordinary as far as he could remember. Pastor McIntosh remembered vividly that on the last visit Leonora had interrupted their conversation. That had happened more than one time. Pastor McIntosh didn't know what to think.

Anita was up late writing a long letter to her son Andrew. Writing to her son was a rewarding experience for her. She found much meaning in relaying to him all the happenings in Yardley Chase, the progress that Jack's Place had been making in introducing new crops such as citrus. She asked Andrew to keep her up to date on the protests, and the advancement of the new political party he was working with to get a voice in the House of Assembly.

At the same time, Anita acknowledged Pastor McIntosh's role in helping him to get started in his political career. She was grateful to him for that. It wasn't her intention to remain silent during their encounter this afternoon. Anita didn't get to say a word as her mother had the right things to say for a brief conversation. Anita didn't mind the short meeting at all. Anita paused while writing the letter, wondering for a moment whether Pastor McIntosh had taken note of that. At first, she was inclined to believe he must have been aware of that, given the fact that they hadn't seen each other for a while. On second thoughts, Anita found it easy to believe that maybe he didn't after all because of Leonora's influence on him. Moreover, all the signs pointed to a visit to Leonora's house. He was coming from that direction; he could have had supper over there. There was also a remote possibility that supper had become a common treat for him at Leonora's.

Lynda didn't mention anything about her silence. In all likelihood, she didn't notice that. It was either that, or Lynda was trying to send a message to Pastor McIntosh. Anita finished the letter then went to bed, hoping that another opportunity to see him would present itself soon. In the meantime, she planned to worship at home. She had a strong desire to resist any attempt to start thinking about Jerome again. She must try, no matter how hard it might be.

The sound of hooves brought Pastor McIntosh to his feet early Monday morning. It was nothing short of unusual for someone to ride early to the manse. It must have been something urgent. Pastor McIntosh jumped in his trousers quickly, and splashed some water across his face, while wiping it at the same time. He could hear a knocking on his front door as soon as he buttoned his shirt. There was a sense of urgency in the knocking; they came in quick succession.

Pastor McIntosh could almost hear his heartbeat pounding in his chest. He had become very nervous. The more knocking he heard, wobbly knees and shaking hands gripped his body. Wilfred hated circumstances such as the one he was about to confront. He wished the situation would pass as quickly as it had crept upon him a few seconds ago. That short time appeared like hours.

Residents of Yardley Chase regarded Pastor McIntosh as a kind of a spiritual giant in the church. He was supposed to be well equipped to deal with any fortunate or unfortunate situation. However, in this case, the stark reality of human imperfection was presenting itself.

The moist hands of Pastor McIntosh reached for the doorknob, the heartbeats coming faster with each moment he got closer to knowing what was about to unfold. The door parted slowly to reveal the familiar figure of Leonora Simmonds. Pastor McIntosh first noticed a white handkerchief being held under her nose. Then there were the tears, the swollen eyes, and a very red nose.

Leonora didn't say anything. She just came into his arms sobbing loud enough to alert anyone passing by. Pastor McIntosh hesitated a bit, but allowed Leonora to have her way.

"What's wrong?" he asked her quickly.

It took Leonora thirty seconds to answer because the manner in which she was crying made it difficult for her to speak. "Dad...Dad...Dad...Dad..." she said, bursting out in uncontrollable bawling.

"What about him?"

Pastor McIntosh had to wait again before she answered. She gripped his arms very tightly, not wanting to let go. "He...H-He..."

"Yes."

"H-He...He's d-dead...dead."

"Dead? How? What do you mean? Where is he?" he asked, releasing her grip on his hand.

I found...him stiff...cold...cold. He wasn't moving...cold, cold," she blurted out with a loud sob.

"My goodness! This isn't happening again! Let's go!" he said, fixing his shirt as they went through the door.

The news about the doctor's death started to spread after

Sally and Jerry came to the manse to start doing some work. Yardley Chase had lost its second important figure in less than six months. Apparently, the doctor was felled by some kind of malady that rendered his heart incapable of carrying out its bodily functions.

Dr. Simmonds was buried the following day. Although he took up residence in Yardley Chase a few months ago, his funeral was well attended. Many people had never met him before.

"Dad always told me he'd never reach seventy. In fact, he always maintained that he would die young," Leonora said to Pastor McIntosh, after the funeral was over and people had started to leave.

"How old was he?" he asked.

"Sixty-eight."

"He was past retirement?"

"He came to Jamaica to retire and to help out the community whenever he could."

"He was doing a fine job," Pastor McIntosh said, wondering how long it would be before she started crying again.

"He knew he was going to die. A few days ago, he told me he had made his last will and testament."

"How will you manage?"

"I'm well taken care of because my father worked very hard to ensure I would be able to get by if he died young or suddenly. He bought property in Kingston and here. We have enough savings to carry us through for many years."

"I know now may not be the right time to ask..."

"Go ahead," Leonora said.

"Will you stay in Yardley Chase or you may move to Kingston?"

"That will depend on a lot of things," she said, not giving any explanation.

Anita, Lynda and John were at the funeral. Anita was by herself a few times, hoping to approach Leonora to offer her condolences. After the funeral service, she was about to approach her but Pastor McIntosh beat her to it. Anita waited until they had stopped talking before she joined her.

"I'm sorry about Dr. Simmonds," she said to her by the graveside where she was standing.

"I guess both of us have something in common, having lost our fathers in such a short time," Leonora said calmly.

"I think you're right. They both died suddenly and that's the hurtful part of it."

"My father was a good man, a good doctor. May the Good Lord have mercy on him."

"I didn't get to know him that well. From what I have heard, though, he was a very kind man," Anita remarked.

"He was a kind man. It's such a pity he couldn't have done much more for these poor people."

"What will you do after all of this?" Anita asked, genuinely concerned about her welfare.

"My father provided for me for many years to come. I'm his only child. Most of his investments are in Kingston."

"Will you move there?" Anita never intended to ask that question; somehow it slipped from out of her mouth. The last thing Anita wanted to do was to give the impression that she was interested in knowing whether Leonora would leave Yardley Chase.

"I like it here. I like it very much...thoughts of leaving haven't entered my mind," she assured her.

Leonora's answer was like rubbing salt into Anita's wound. It would've been better for Anita never to ask that question. "Most of the newcomers to this area often end up liking it. I can't blame them because it's very nice here," Anita said politely.

"I'm one of them," Leonora said, managing a smile.

"I wonder what those two are talking about so long?" Lynda asked John.

"I would expect that Anita is offering her condolences. From there, the argument could go on to anything," John suggested.

"I hope it doesn't turn into a quarrel," Lynda said jokingly.

"Quarrel? What would they be fussing about?" John asked, far from being amused.

"Anything, you know women all over, especially when they are pretty. They're always competing against each other," she said.

"Ha! Ha! That's a nice way of putting it. In Yardley Chase, there's hardly anyone to compete for. I'm taken," he boasted.

"You must be a happy man, John. I'm glad for you. It didn't work out with Anita...there could be a good reason for that. Here you have found a woman that I know will make you a good wife."

"Thank you, Lynda, I'm confident she will, too. It's my sincere wish that Anita will find the person of her dreams."

"She may have found him already."

"Where is he?" John asked, looking around the immediate surroundings.

"You know what I mean."

"Oh! For a moment I was about to jump for joy to learn she has found someone worthy of marriage."

"You really mean her that well, John, after she has hurt you?"

"Put it this way. Although she had no desire for me, Anita did find Elizabeth. That, I'm grateful for, and will forever remember her for that."

"I can see you have a change of heart, John. It's very refreshing to know."

"Who's this person?" John asked, almost convinced he had the same person in mind.

"I'll allow time to reveal that person." Lynda smiled.

John wasn't looking in the direction of Anita and Leonora. Lynda saw Pastor McIntosh heading in their direction as Anita was walking from Leonora and was coming in their direction. Because of the distance between them, there was no way Pastor McIntosh could catch up to Anita before she reached where they were standing. Acting like an intruder, Lynda turned in the direction of Pastor McIntosh, hoping Anita would follow.

"Let's go to have a word with Pastor," Lynda told John. "Have you perfected your practice for the wedding as yet?"

"I may need a few more hours," he sighed.

"Well, let's see what he says."

It took them less than a minute to reach Pastor McIntosh.

"Glad you could make it," Pastor McIntosh said, extending his hand.

"We've been through this and know the pain," Lynda said. "Support is very important in times like this."

"How true? A funeral, a wedding—all in one week, John?"

"Yes, sir. That's what life is all about, isn't it? You were born, get married, die."

"Indeed, life is a vapor," Pastor McIntosh said.

Lynda kept looking around, hoping to see Anita joining them. Her eyes combed the funeral ground until they stopped where five people stood closely together in the far corner near the entrance. Lynda couldn't believe her eyes. Hugging Anita was her son Andrew; standing beside Andrew was Elizabeth. Lynda got John's attention by jerking him by his sleeve.

"Look," she said, pointing in the direction where they were standing.

A wide grin, followed by a laugh, transformed John's face. "Wooo! Look who's here, the bride herself...Look at her, isn't she gorgeous?"

"You'll be getting a good wife, John. I have known her for many years and believe me you'll see for yourself."

"Come," John said commandingly, indicating for them to follow him. They walked over to where they were. Andrew was the first to run to greet his grandmother.

"I'm really glad to be here, Grandma."

"Thanks, son, it is good to see you, too."

"It's good to be in Yardley Chase again," Elizabeth said, giving John and Pastor McIntosh a hug.

"Hi, Pastor McIntosh...John, I couldn't miss this wedding. Elizabeth and John have been good to me. I thought what better way to honor them than to be here."

"You never made a better decision," Anita said.

"We were shocked to learn of another death in Yardley Chase. I never knew Dr. Simmonds, but from what I've been hearing, he was a nice man."

"He was indeed," Pastor McIntosh said.

Pastor McIntosh and Lynda were standing about three feet apart. Anita, trying to avoid him, was standing on the other side beside Andrew, John and Elizabeth.

It was the only little gathering left on the funeral ground. It had caught Leonora's attention. She saw Elizabeth and decided to go over there.

"I'm sorry...we share in your grief," Elizabeth said, greeting her.

"Thank you."

"I never met your father. I understand he was a very nice man," Andrew interjected.

"You must be Andrew."

"I am."

"Well, thank you, Andrew, for your kind words. How's Kingston?"

"Pretty nice, only a bit too hot sometimes."

"At least we have the cool breeze from Lover's Leap around here."

"I miss Yardley Chase terribly...I'll always miss it."

"Well, it's time to go, Andrew and Elizabeth, you must be very tired," Anita said.

"Indeed, we are," said Elizabeth. John looked at her and smiled.

"Good night, everyone," Anita said, leading the way out.

Leonora and Pastor McIntosh remained behind. Again, Anita had said nothing to him. As much as he wanted to say something to her, the opportunity never came. Pastor McIntosh was convinced this time that something had gone wrong—terribly wrong.

No one else noticed that they hadn't said a word except Lynda. Anita was very happy to see her son. That was all that mattered to her.

Andrew dropped a bombshell over dinner later that evening. He had been approached to contest a seat for the House of Assembly. The two women around the table with him sprang simultaneously out of their seats to hug him tightly, laughing and jumping for joy.

"Oh my goodness! Oh my goodness! I can't believe it! I can't believe it!" yelled Anita.

"Oh, Andrew! I'm thrilled for you! You're going to win!"

"Really?" he said, blushing.

"How did you accomplish that in such a short time?" Anita asked.

"I work very hard. To be honest with you, I work day and night. That has paid off in the long run."

"Where will you be contesting the seat?" Lynda asked.

"In east Kingston," Andrew said reluctantly. "I made it clear to them that the next time I want to contest it will be in the southern section of this parish."

"Good. When is it going to take place?" Anita asked.

"Next year, about June."

"We'll all be there to support you, my son."

"I'm looking forward to that. I sometimes get nervous and impatient. Soon, I'll have to start doing a lot of reading on politics."

"Will you need some money?" Lynda asked.

Andrew appreciated that question very much because he didn't know how to ask it. "As a matter of fact, I'll need some money for that."

"Well, your grandfather gave you his blessings before he left us, and we have enough to help you out in whatever way you need it."

Andrew stepped in front of Lynda and hugged her again. "Thank you, Grandma. I certainly appreciate it."

Anita watched them, a sparkle of satisfaction in her eyes.

Jack's Place came alive with the movements of machetes and hoes on Wednesday morning. Preparation for the wedding of John and Elizabeth had started to make everyone around a busybody. The lawn had to be cut, the hedges trimmed, a booth had to be constructed from coconut leaves, and a make-shift fireplace outside to accommodate the huge pots for the cooking of the meals.

John started the preparation from early morning. He worked right into the night. Elizabeth was by his side most of the time. This made John feel as if he was on top of the world. Imagine, he had a woman for himself; maybe it was time to sing praises to God for making his dreams become a reality.

"You're going to make me the happiest husband on earth," John told Elizabeth when he was ready to call it a day.

"I'd like to echo that statement, except to insert wife rather than husband," Elizabeth chuckled.

"Are you getting nervous?"

"Who wouldn't be? Sometimes I wish it to be two weeks away in order to enjoy the pleasure of looking forward to it. On the other hand, sometimes I wish we had done it already."

"You know we both are thinking the same way. Hmm, that's a good sign we'll live happily ever after," John said.

"I wonder what could ever make us unhappy."

"When we realize we're growing old together, even then, we should be happy we have each other to depend on," John said soberly.

"You are right. God will be on our side, remember?" Elizabeth said, pointing a finger into the sky.

"I was telling myself today that I truly have to thank God for this blessing of sending me a wife. I have to start attending church, Elizabeth. That's a pledge I've made to myself. I have every intention of fulfilling that wish."

Elizabeth came up to give him a hug. "Thank you, John; thank you, dear Father," she whispered.

Pastor McIntosh, too, had been working hard all day. He sat in his living room sipping tea, trying to relax. He was exhausted and thoughts of canceling the Wednesday night prayer meeting came across his mind several times. A duty is a duty, he told himself; regardless of the circumstances, he would have the meeting.

Anita! Why had she stopped coming to prayer meeting? At the outset, she was there first every Wednesday evening. Lately, she was hardly at services, and whenever she did, Anita disappeared as soon as it was over. What was wrong? He could only hope everything was fine with her. Her father's death must have left some deep emotional scars—much more than he could imagine.

A sudden tap on the door got his attention. Pastor McIntosh was getting used to people calling on him all hours of the night. The evening was pretty young, thus a knock wasn't out of the ordinary.

Leonora stood in the doorway; the look on her face was rather troubling. It reminded him of her reaction to Dr. Simmonds' death last week.

"Come on in...is everything alright," Pastor McIntosh asked, his voice trembling a bit.

Instead of stepping past him, Leonora turned to cuddle into his arms as her sobbing permeated the quiet room, disrupting the long silence. Pastor McIntosh could do nothing but to hold her. She clung to him not wanting to let go. Pastor McIntosh wanted to get out of that awkward position, despite Leonora's obvious need to be held by someone.

"Hold me for a while, please," she said softly between sobs.

"Is everything okay?" he asked again.

"I need to...to talk to someone. I can't..." Leonora started to cry again. This time, Pastor McIntosh led her to the couch, helping her to sit down.

"Sit here...let's talk. It's been difficult for you. I know that. You lost your father, now you feel like you are alone in this world."

Leonora nodded in agreement.

"We're all here to give you support. The church is here; that's why it's here to nurture, to help all of us in our hour of need."

"I never knew it would be like this," Leonora mumbled, trying to regain her composure. Her watery eyes glittered in the lamplight, a symbol of pity and empathy to any onlooker.

"Death is the enemy of all of us. We all look forward to that day when we'll overcome it like our Savior did. I was having some tea, would you like some?"

"Thank you."

Another knock came from the door. "Hmm, it seems I'm having a busy evening." He smiled, trying to cheer up Leonora.

"Andrew!" he blurted out, opening the door to allow him in. "It's good to see you," he said, shaking his hand.

Andrew didn't see Leonora at first. He tried tactfully to hide his astonishment when he recognized her.

"Oh! Hi, Leonora, it's good to see you," he said, a barrage of ideas invading his mind.

"Hi, Andrew."

"I went to church for prayer meeting..."

"My, my...Oh! I'm late...I had such a tough day that I almost forgot about tonight," Pastor McIntosh admitted, grabbing his jacket that was hanging behind a chair.

"Some people are waiting. I told them I would come to see if everything was fine with you."

"I'm fine. I was in counseling with Leonora here and the time slipped by quickly."

Andrew wondered about that, trying to dismiss any notion he had about the reason for Leonora's presence there. The woman lost her father a few weeks ago; a counseling session was in order. Andrew's only reason for arriving at such a conclusion was Anita's admission to him that she had stopped coming to church. Andrew was baffled because Anita had become a zealot up to the time when he was living in Yardley Chase. Presently, she was far from that. As much as Andrew tried, Anita wouldn't give any reasons for that, except to say she was taking a break from the church.

Leonora's presence tonight gave Andrew something to think about. It was difficult for Andrew not to think about a possible relationship between the pastor and this young, beautiful girl, who was alone in the world.

The usual Wednesday night faces were waiting for Pastor. The face he searched for as soon as he took his place behind the pulpit wasn't there. Pastor McIntosh was disappointed that Anita wasn't present. He had wrongfully assumed that she had accompanied Andrew.

Leonora was back to her normal self, taking her seat in the front row. Andrew sat at the back, not far from Sally. The prayer meeting lasted for about an hour. Sally came to join him when it was over.

"Lookin' forward to di wedding?" she teased.

"I have to admit I'm doing that. How are you doing, Sally?"

"Fine, Massa Andrew, fine. How is Miss Anita, sah? She not comin' again?"

"Hmmm. You haven't seen her recently?"

"Not at all, sah. She used to be here every week," Sally said.

"She'll be back soon."

"Miss Leonora is always busy; she could do with some help around here."

"Busy? You mean with Sunday school?" Andrew asked, looking at Leonora talking to Pastor McIntosh up at the front.

"Everything, sah. She's in charge here...excep' for Pastor," Sally said jokingly.

Andrew used his political wit to have a better picture of what was going on. Leonora's dominance in the church, and preoccupation with Pastor, must have something to do with Anita's sudden lack of interest.

"It seems she works very hard to get things going, though."

"True, sah, true...she works hard all di time. I'm sure Pastor must notice dat, too, sah."

Andrew got a hint Sally had been observing the situation, too. "Everyone must be noticing."

"I only hope dem nat talkin'."

"Talking about what?"

"Yuh know, di usual gossip, especially when it involves Pastor." She smiled.

"The church isn't a place for gossip."

"Heh, you find dat in every church, sah."

"Have you heard anything?" Andrew asked.

"Not yet, sah, not yet."

CHAPTER 13

A rather bright half moon hovered in the sky above. It gave enough light to kill the pitch blackness that had made the night not too encouraging for a walk. Stars dominated the Jamaican sky, yet their distance made them of no effect on the dark surroundings.

"It's too dark to ride or walk. You should spend the night here. I'll sleep in the couch," Pastor McIntosh told Leonora after service.

Everyone had left, and they were the only two people to close up the church, at least that was what they thought. From behind an almond tree in the churchyard, two eyes watched intently to see what was happening back there. The figure waited patiently for everyone to leave. The dark night paid off by shielding the figure behind the tree. It arrived there near the end of the prayer meeting and watched strenuously in the dark to identify those who were leaving.

"Thanks, Pastor, I do appreciate that," Leonora said. She was very happy with that invitation. In fact, she was hoping he would suggest that. The thought of her spending another night in that lonely house made her shiver. She hated to think of the lonely nights ahead of her; it was something she had to change quickly. How she would do that was beyond her. Nevertheless, for all intent and purposes, it was something she had to do sooner, rather than later.

Pastor McIntosh fumbled in the dark to ensure that the key was inside the door. He had problems finding the keyhole. Leonora saw his dilemma and moved closer to help, close enough for Pastor McIntosh to hear her breathing.

"It's okay, I'll find it," he assured her.

"Are you certain?"

"Yes, I have it. I should've made sure it was in before I turned off the lantern," Pastor McIntosh said regretfully.

A few feet away, the figure behind the tree could hear bits and pieces of the dialogue. A parted window made it possible. Eyes pierced the dark vehemently to see what was going on. All that greeted those eyes were dull movements that were difficult to decipher.

"Come, let's go," Pastor McIntosh suggested.

The figure behind the tree became very curious about where they would be heading. It moved out of its position to follow them, making quiet and careful steps, trying to keep up with the pace at which they were walking.

At first, the figure thought they were going to head in the direction of Leonora's house. Instead, they went to the manse of Pastor McIntosh. What was happening here? The figure was more curious.

"That was a good meeting tonight, "Leonora said, walking up the steps to the front door. The figure was only a few feet away as it wanted to ensure that what was happening was real. It was real all right.

The figure watched them open the door to go in. The figure crept up beside the front window, stepping on a piece of stick in the process. The stick made a crackling sound that died away quickly in the quiet night. Leonora and Pastor McIntosh couldn't have heard that.

The lantern in the house was already lit. The figure had no problem watching the shadows move about in the front room. They were talking although the figure couldn't make out what was being said. Movements continued in the room for another ten minutes until the light went out. The figure considered several possibilities that could occur in the dark. A cough in the front room changed everything. Someone had made a bed there. The light that came on in another room to the back suggested the other person would be sleeping there.

Andrew couldn't explain his mother's absence from Jack's Place. He came from prayer meeting and before retiring to bed decided to check on Anita to ensure everything was fine. Her bed was empty. Lynda was fast asleep and Andrew didn't want to wake her. A faint smell of alcohol came from his grandmother's room, but Andrew dismissed the thought of her drinking, as soon as it had entered his mind. The loud snoring from Lynda reminded him of his tiredness.

Andrew made a cup of tea and sat around the table in the kitchen. Anita walked through the front door hastily, unaware of his presence.

"Having a late walk, Mom?" Andrew shouted from the kitchen.

The sound of Anita's footsteps going up the stairs changed pace, indicating she was coming back down and heading for the kitchen. She came inside, sitting down in front of Andrew.

"I wanted to get out of the house…decided to go for a walk." She yawned.

"Why didn't you come to prayer meeting? That would have got you out of the house and, furthermore, you never miss prayer meeting."

"I was there, Andrew…in spirit." Anita smiled. She wanted to tell him that to get rid of Jerome's haunting images, she decided to go there, but concluded that wouldn't be a good idea. As far as Andrew was concerned, Anita had already gotten over Jerome. She wanted them to continue thinking that way.

"Is everything going well with you at church?" Andrew inquired, searching her face for an answer.

"I haven't been there for a while," Anita said dryly.

"Why? You were quite zealous when I was here."

"I'm taking a break for a while. I'll be back."

"The church needs all the support it can get. Pastor

McIntosh works very hard to get things moving in order to serve everyone in the community."

"Leonora works hard, too."

"So that's it, Mom."

"What?"

"Leonora, of course. She's the reason you haven't been going to church. I'm beginning to get concerned about you, Mom," Andrew said, reaching across the table to hold her hand.

"What are you talking about?" Anita noted the expression on her son's face and knew he had cornered her. They've had such a good relationship over the years that it made no sense to deny anything. Andrew was the only person she could discuss most of her concerns and challenges.

"Leonora is going head over heels over Pastor and has been working endlessly to get his attention."

"She has been very successful with that," Anita hinted.

"How?"

"She is even sleeping at his house."

"Sleeping? Where did you get that from?"

"With my own eyes," Anita assured Andrew. "I saw them tonight."

Andrew's eyes seemed to be popping out of his head. "You were at church?"

"Not church, I was on the compound," Anita corrected him.

"You mean you were watching what was going on after church."

"Exactly, son. I wanted to see for myself what that woman has been up to these last days. I know the death of her father has earned her a lot of sympathy from Wilfred. Knowing her, I believe she's making use of that."

"I agree. What are you going to do about that?" Andrew asked.

"Only time will tell, son. Let's go to get some sleep."

Leonora must have been the first person to rise in Yardley Chase next morning. To avoid any controversy, she woke up early, got dressed and rode back to her house. She knew that staying by the manse was highly inappropriate, although her circumstances merited such a kind gesture from Pastor.

Leonora didn't sleep well last night. She started to devise a plan in her head about where life should be going for her. It would only be a matter of time before she had to choose between Yardley Chase and somewhere else, most likely Kingston, where her father had investments that belonged to her. Her future rested in the hands of Pastor Wilfred McIntosh.

She had been trying desperately to seduce him. Leonora respected his integrity and dedication to God. However, that didn't mean she should give up on him. All she was asking was to have a relationship that would eventually lead to marriage.

Leonora was hoping Anita's absence from church would have made things better for her. She had to wonder if that had made matters worse. What was truly the reason for her absence, though? The question tickled her brain as doubt crept into her mind. What was bothering her was whether her actions at church had any real effect on Anita's decision to stop attending church. Guilt trickled into her thoughts and it made her begin to despise her actions. Notwithstanding all of that, Leonora forced herself to believe that she should have no regrets. It was worth the effort. She didn't believe she had committed any sins. Nothing happened. And if her hunch was right, Pastor McIntosh didn't appear interested one bit.

After Leonora had left, Pastor McIntosh slipped into another of his thought processes—something he had been doing quite often, especially when Anita was involved.

Wilfred wanted to go right over to Jack's Place and ask Anita what had gone wrong. He wished he had the guts to do that. To think of it, he should have no problem facing up to such a challenge because that was his job. The exception, though, seemed to be in this case.

Leonora was putting the pressure on him to enter into some kind of relationship. At first, Wilfred didn't want to admit what his sixth sense was telling him. It became evident over the past few weeks that she was searching for companionship; it was confirmed when she came to the manse last night.

Relationships had become a kind of anathema to Wilfred since his last serious relationship in England, and his entry into the ministry. Whenever he thought of it, he became wary and imagined all the negative possibilities.

Wilfred dismissed those thoughts quickly, preferring to steer them to the big day on Saturday, when John and Elizabeth would be exchanging marriage vows. Wilfred was happy for both of them. They deserved each other.

One thing Wilfred was positive about was that Anita would be there. Somehow, it looked like an insurmountable task to perform under the watchful eyes of Anita. Why should he feel like that anyway? They had shared many ideas during the period she had been coming to church, and that memorable trip into Kingston.

He guessed he would be in an awkward position performing such a significant rite in the home of someone who seemed to be avoiding him. Was Anita avoiding him, or vice versa? If he was, Wilfred wasn't conscious about that. Suppose Anita had more serious problems that had nothing to do with church? That was a distinct possibility. On that note, Wilfred decided to let the matter rest—for now.

Anita had an unexpected visitor on Friday afternoon. Peter Bradley saw Anita under the star apple tree, the relic of the former Hell House, and rode up to greet her. Peter knew the history of Hell House and that Anita had her first encounter there with the slave Jerome. What was she thinking? It would almost be a guarantee that her presence there would usher in memories of the past.

"Good afternoon," Peter said politely.

"Good afternoon, Peter," Anita answered, looking around at people busy preparing for the wedding tomorrow. "How are you?" She had seen him coming through the gate and was neither happy nor sad that Peter was there.

"I'm fine, Anita. How about you?" He smiled warmly.

"I'm getting along. I thought you had forgotten us."

"I've been busy working with some new clients. I have some things to discuss with Lynda. I also wanted to come for the wedding and here I am." He grinned sheepishly.

"Well, glad you could make it. Everyone is getting excited around here as the big day approaches."

"Who wouldn't be?"

"How's Black River doing these days?" Anita asked, looking in the direction from where a small gust of wind was blowing.

"Black River is fine, although I do get frustrated sometimes."

"You shouldn't be; don't you have enough work to keep you occupied?"

"If it wasn't for that, it would have been worse. How's Andrew doing?" Peter asked, deliberately changing the argument.

"As a matter of fact he's here with us." She smiled.

"How come?"

"He came to look for us and to be at the wedding."

"Hmmm, this wedding is shaping up to be a big one."

"They both deserve it. Have you eaten?"

"I could do well with some food. It looks like they'll be cooking a whole cow here tomorrow," Peter said, pointing to a pile of wood nearby.

"Ha! Don't be surprised if they do that. It's cool out here; stay and let me fetch you something," Anita said, taking his bag and heading for the house.

Such a wonderful woman, Peter said to himself. Peter wished they were getting married tomorrow.

He observed Andrew walking in his direction, and pretended he didn't notice.

"Hi, Peter! It's good to see you," Andrew yelled above the noise from the chopping of wood and the hum of voices that was assembling wood for tomorrow's big cooking. He came over to shake his hand.

"I'm doing fine...you look pretty good."

"Thanks," Andrew said, blushing. "I assume you're here for tomorrow's big day."

"I'm ready. It's truly going to be a big day. I'm glad to be here."

"Glad you could make it."

"What's happening over there in Kingston?"

"Kingston is great! It's living up to my expectations. Did you hear I'm running for a seat in the House of Assembly next year?" Andrew asked alarmingly.

"No...hmmm, you're truly stepping up. I'm very proud of you...the whole of Yardley Chase and this parish," Peter said, reaching out for his hand to shake it again.

"I haven't won yet," Andrew reminded him.

"You will, I can assure you."

"I need the encouragement."

Anita returned with a tray full of food.

"What do we have here that smells awfully good?" Peter asked.

"Open and you will see," Anita said cheerfully, removing the covering to reveal rice, vegetables and beef.

Peter rested the tray in his lap, wasting no time to devour what was placed before him.

Two hours later, nightfall captured Yardley Chase, dissolving any trace of the sun with its dark fangs. It was the night before John and Elizabeth's memorable day, and there was excitement at Jack's Place.

No one had slept that night. Jack's Place was too busy. The animals had just been slaughtered; the meat was being prepared for cooking the moment the sun's first rays peeped from behind the Spur Tree Hills. Inside the house, Lynda's kitchen and living room were packed with people. Pastor McIntosh was missing out on the fun. He was the last one to get there.

Anita saw when he came in. She made no effort to greet him, instead she kept on talking with Peter, and by so doing, resisted any attempt to let her thoughts stray to Jerome. Whenever she thought or heard of a wedding, their forbidden love was recalled with little difficulty.

Pastor McIntosh saw Anita, too, making no move toward her either. Chatter and laughter filled the whole room. Everyone appeared to be in a world of enjoyment to themselves.

Lynda saw Pastor McIntosh standing by himself.

"Isn't this lovely?" Lynda said, referring to the throng of people in her house.

"This is how a wedding should be—happy and full of laughter," Pastor McIntosh said, his eyes occasionally focusing on Anita. Pastor McIntosh wasn't certain what had been overcoming him each time he cast his eyes in her direction.

Somehow, he started to get those feelings of years gone by when he was involved in a relationship back in England. Why was he feeling that way?

"Are you okay?" Lynda asked him. She had noticed his gaze in that direction, and picked up that there was something of interest to him.

"Uh, I...I'm okay. I'm a little tired. In addition to that I'm getting rather anxious about tomorrow. Weddings are usually like that for me."

"Who wouldn't be?"

John, with Elizabeth under his arms, came over to them, smiles all over their faces.

"As soon as I'm ready I'll let you know," John teased.

"I'm very happy for you two, you deserve each other. I'll wait on you to give the cue, John," he laughed.

One by one the crowd drifted away. At midnight, it was only Lynda, Anita, Elizabeth, Peter and Andrew who remained in the house. Anita and Peter remained locked in their talking position. They never moved from their position. Pastor McIntosh, even though he wanted to, made no intrusion into their conversation. Anita laughed and talked with Peter all night. That sent Pastor McIntosh home with something to think about.

Pastor McIntosh had learned several lessons from tonight. One, Anita was a happy woman, two, she was totally ignoring him. But why?

Saturday morning was as bright as could be. A mixture of sun and clouds decorated the early morning hours. By ten o' clock, though, it was mostly sun, except for a few clouds that dotted the horizon looking across from Lover's Leap.

A vast sea of black and white dominated the grounds of Yardley Chase Baptist Church, with the wedding ceremony only minutes away. It was a sight to behold. The entire district must have come out for this wedding. The church was tested for its size; people crammed into it to be a part of the service, while those who couldn't get a foot in, peeped through windows, doors, crevices, openings, in order to get a glimpse of the proceedings. Even former slaves who worked under the watchful eyes of John during slavery stood on the other side of the church grounds to watch what was happening.

The front row in the church was occupied by Lynda, Anita, Peter, two deacons and of course Leonora. The bridal party stayed on the other side.

Anita had to admit she was very impressed with Pastor McIntosh's conduct at the ceremony. He remained calm, was all smiles, his choice of words was right on. Instead of looking at the bride and groom, Anita's eyes never left him. She remembered last night how she deliberately avoided him. Anita told herself he must come to her; she wouldn't go to him, even though he was a guest in her house. He never did. Since last night, Anita had been asking herself what had actually gone wrong.

A few feet away from her stood the immaculately dressed Leonora. Her eyes, too, were pasted on Pastor. All Leonora could wish for was the day she would stand beside him to exchange vows.

The ceremony lasted for less than an hour. The crowd started to drift into Jack's Place for the part of the wedding most people were looking forward to—eating and drinking. There was enough for the more than three hundred people who graced the lawns of Jack's Place.

John and Elizabeth were the perfect match. John jokingly pinched himself several times to prove he wasn't dreaming. He had in fact become a husband to a wonderful Christian woman, who had been helping him to deal with his own spirituality. In addition, she had given John a sense of worth.

Anita and Peter sat at the reception table, but far from Pastor McIntosh. Whoever was responsible for the table might have done that innocently. Andrew sat between Lynda and Anita, while Pastor McIntosh sat beside John and his new bride.

From where Anita was sitting, it was difficult to see Pastor

McIntosh. That made it easier for Anita who thought it best not to keep glancing at him. Although Leonora wasn't at the head table, she was only a few feet away from her. She must have deliberately chosen the nearest seat to the head table.

The speeches came and went by but the food and drink lingered on. Everyone was having a good time, except for one person—Pastor McIntosh. He excused himself from around the table the moment he saw Anita do that. He trailed her to the corner of the house where a group of children were gathered for play. Anita wanted some fresh air, telling Peter she would soon be back.

An awareness of someone's presence forced her to turn around from where she was standing. Leonora watched from the far corner of the house where she, too, had been trailing both of them.

Pastor McIntosh was standing in front of her, a warm and friendly smile on his face. Anita started to smile, too, suspecting that what was to come would be her triumph or defeat.

"I'm wondering how long you're going to avoid me," he said simply.

"I'm wondering how long you're going to ignore me," Anita replied.

"I guess we are both guilty of something."

"I agree, we're both guilty of something," Anita said, taking a step closer to him.

"I know I'm guilty of one thing," Pastor McIntosh hinted.

"What's that?"

"Anita," he said, reaching for her hand and holding it in his, "the only thing I'm guilty of doing is taking too long to recognize that I'm in love...with you..."

Suddenly, as if she had been waiting to hear those words, Anita started to cry. She squeezed his hand, allowing it to go around his waist. The next thing she knew he was holding her, the first time he ever did that.

"I've loved you all along...all along," she sobbed. "It was...it was so painful at one point..."

"I'm sorry. I've been a fool not to have noticed that."

Anita squeezed him tighter, and looking across his shoulder she could clearly see another small gathering watching everything that was going on between them. The first people she saw were Leonora and Peter standing close together, then there were Andrew, Lynda, John and Elizabeth. There was one loud clap from John, followed by Andrew. And they all started to clap louder and louder.

"I guess they're asking when the next big wedding is," Pastor McIntosh said.

"Anytime you're ready." Anita smiled. "I'm the happiest woman in Yardley Chase," Anita said, tears crawling down her cheeks.

"I agree because I'm the happiest man around," Pastor McIntosh said with almost a laugh.

Anita took one quick look across the peak at Lover's Leap. "A new day is dawning," she said aloud. Deep inside Anita whispered, "Goodbye, Jerome, until we meet again."

Printed in the United States
79817LV00006B/132

9 781413 784046